THE MATH INSPECTORS

MYSTERY, ADVENTURE, HUMOR... and MATH!

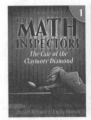   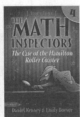

Praise for the Math Inspectors:

"Clever, humorous, and well-written detective mystery series for elementary and middle school readers. The plot kept me guessing and entertained." - B.M.

"This is a fun math series for the eight to tween set with well developed characters who could jump onto the Saturday morning TV screen and find a comfortable home on PBS." - C.Q.

"I bought this for my 10 year-old son who is a voracious reader   and loves mysteries, and he just loves the series. It makes math a fun challenge, not a chore, and still managed to entertain my bright child!" -R.B.

WANT TWO FREE STORIES?

SIGN UP FOR MY NO-SPAM NEWSLETTER
AND GET TWO DANIEL KENNEY STORIES,
PLUS ALWAYS BE THE FIRST TO KNOW
ABOUT NEW CONTENT.

ALL FOR FREE.

DETAILS CAN BE FOUND
AT THE END OF THIS BOOK.

THE MATH INSPECTORS

BOOK THREE
The Case of the Christmas Caper

Daniel Kenney & Emily Boever

TRENDWOODPRESS

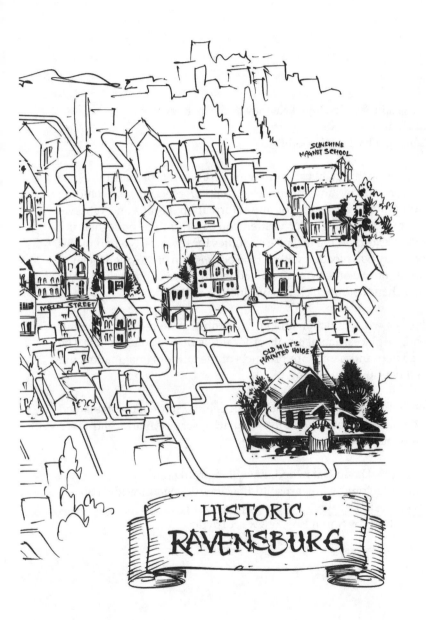

Editing by David Gatewood, www.lonetrout.com
Interior Layout by Polgarus Studios, www.polgarusstudio.com
Cover Design by www.AuthorSupport.com
Illustrations by Sumit Roy, www.scorpydesign.com

Table of Contents

CHAPTER ONE

DECEMBER 23, 3:14 P.M.

The heavy door creaked open. Prisoner 37066 had only been in this room once before, but knew to sit down at the table and wait for the call that was sure to come.

The phone rang only once before it was snatched up.

"What's taking so long?" snapped the prisoner.

"Patience, patience," said the voice on the other end of the line.

"Your boss promised me a transfer if I fixed the plan. I answered all of the stupid questions you guys have thrown at me, so why haven't you held up your end of the bargain?"

"This may come as a shock," said the caller, "but undermining the legal system in order to transfer a convicted fraud to lighter security takes time, even for the Boss."

"I doubt that," said the prisoner. "And I don't want to spend Christmas in this place."

"Good," said the caller, "because I am holding your transfer orders in my hand right now. You can be in a minimum security facility this time tomorrow, just in time to hang up your stockings for Christmas Eve."

The prisoner laughed coldly. "Why do I get the feeling I still need to do something else before those orders are delivered?"

"Now that you mention it," said the caller, "there *is* one more thing the Boss needs to know. You have lived in Ravensburg your whole life, so tell me: when will the kids start gathering on Main Street tomorrow morning?"

"That's easy. When I was a kid, we'd—" Something clicked in the prisoner's mind. All of the caller's random questions about the plans suddenly fell into place. In one agonizing moment, the truth came. "Wait a minute! You guys are going to—but you can't! No, I'm not going to let you do that to—"

"Be very careful what you say next," said the voice on the phone. "This is a one-time deal, and it expires in sixty seconds. Answer my question, and you will be on a transfer bus within the hour. Refuse, and you will stay where you are for the next decade. What will it be?"

The prisoner leaned both elbows on the table and thought hard. All those other things before were illegal, but this... this was different. This was—the cops had to be warned! Then again, answering one more little question wasn't actually committing the crime. One simple question. And this place was unbearable. Wouldn't anybody in this situation choose the same thing?

The old clock on the wall said there were fifteen seconds left. Ten. Five.

Prisoner 37066 made a decision.

CHAPTER TWO

A CHRISTMAS EVE TRADITION

"Stanley Robinson Carusoe," said Gertie as she leaned across the booth at Mabel's Diner and watched Stanley scribble numbers on a pad of paper. "You're doing math on Christmas Eve? You've got problems."

Stanley pushed his glasses up the bridge of his nose. "Correction, Gertie. I've got *one* problem, and it's really starting to bug me."

"But why even worry about Mr. Beagle's extra credit challenge when you've already got over 100% in math class? Do you need any help?"

"I don't think so. I can figure this out on my own."

"Suit yourself," said Gertie. She returned to her

conversation with Charlotte and Felix. "What'd you call it again?" she asked Felix.

Felix was balancing a wadded-up napkin on his fork. "It's called a Kid-A-Pult," he said. "You strap in, pull the lever, and the thing launches you like fifty feet. I want one."

Charlotte folded her arms. "That's impossible."

"Not if you wear a *helmet*." Felix demonstrated by flinging his fork into action.

Charlotte took the shot between the eyes without blinking. She let out a low growl. "If that ever happens again..."

"I'll experience a slow and agonizing death?"

Charlotte drummed her fingers on the table. "Just so long as we understand each other." She pointed out the frosted window of the friends' favorite corner booth. "Anyway, what I meant is it's impossible for you to know what's behind those doors."

Stanley looked up from his math problem to follow the line of Charlotte's finger down the street to an old brick building with an ancient hand-carved wooden sign.

"Charlotte's right," said Stanley, turning back to his numbers. "It's not possible."

Felix went to work wadding up another napkin. "I'm telling you, there's a Kid-A-Pult in there. This kid in my gym class, his mother overheard the postman telling his grandma's neighbor all about it." Felix pulled back his fork and flipped it forward. This time the paper cannonball hit someone else between the eyes.

"Ouch!" Gertie cried. She rubbed her nose, then swung at Felix over the table. Her short arms didn't come close to touching him. "But how did..." she stammered, "whoever we're talking about, get past all the crazy, top-secret security systems? The lie detectors? The alligators?"

Gertie's Silver Dollar Pancakes arrived. She offered the familiar waitress a smile. "Thanks, Mabel."

Mabel set down the syrup and smiled back. "What did I forget? Need extra butter?"

"That's it!" said Stanley.

"That's what?" Gertie asked.

"Extra butter. I mean extra stuff—my math problem—never mind."

Stanley quickly finished his calculations. In the end, the solution was simple—but the problem *looked* complicated because it contained a lot of extra information that Stanley *thought* was important to the problem. Turns out it never was. Mr. Beagle, Stanley's math teacher, liked to call that kind of information *superfluous information.*

Stanley laid his pencil down, looked at the others, and sighed. "Okay, *now* I can concentrate on Christmas." He spotted the breakfast combo platter in front of him for the first time and pulled it closer. As always, he tossed the blueberry muffin to Charlotte.

Gertie poured maple syrup onto her plate and shook her head. "Like I said, Stanley, you've got problems. So, to catch you up on our spirited conversation, it's now Charlotte's turn to tell us what *she* thinks is in Mr. Douglas's basement."

Charlotte set the muffin down and folded her hands. "I've already told you, it's impossible to know. While Mr. Douglas doesn't keep alligators in a pit, like Gertie seems to think, everyone knows there are trap doors in that place that lead to a dungeon."

"A dungeon?" Stanley said.

Charlotte shrugged. "Yeah, where trespassers are kept until they die."

Stanley laughed. "Mr. Douglas's Toy Store does not have alligators, an old dungeon, or anything else dark and scary."

"You *would* believe that," Gertie scoffed through a mouthful of pancakes.

As the noise from the crowd outside grew, Stanley and his friends turned to stare out the window at the old building once more. Set between the First Bank of Ravensburg and Graham's General Store, Mr. Douglas's Toy Store didn't look like anything special. Its faded red brick façade matched every other building on Main Street. But two details made it stand out. First, outside this particular building hung a beautifully carved wooden sign reading *Douglas and Sons, Toys for All Ages*. And second, at the moment its tall narrow windows were covered with padlocked green shutters.

Felix cleared his throat. "It's not that I'm complaining or anything, Mabel," he shouted toward the front counter, "but munching on these paper menus only tides a guy over for so long."

Mabel rolled her eyes as she came their way. "Your breakfast will be wheeled out momentarily, Your Highness. You *did* order the entire left side of the menu, after all. That takes time."

Felix shook his head. "I did no such thing. I purposely left the blueberry crepes out just to shake things up."

Mabel's nostrils flared as she set a steaming plate of grits in front of Charlotte. "It's on the house, dear."

Charlotte smiled and shook her head. "Thanks,

Mabel, but that's really not necessary."

"Sure it is. I mean—anyway, Merry Christmas, Charlotte. And besides... well, I'll let you kids get back to discussing the latest toy rumors. But I'm telling you it's no use. Stanley's right about one thing: Douglas's place doesn't lead to trap doors or alligators or any such nonsense."

Stanley made a face at his friends. "See?"

"Truth is," Mabel continued, "anybody who's anybody knows that a pack of werewolves keeps those toys safe and secret, and that's the way it's been as far back as anybody can remember."

Stanley shook his head at Mabel, who just winked at him.

But despite his scepticism, Stanley knew that Douglas's Toy Store was no normal toy store. It had secrets.

For one thing, every year on the day after Thanksgiving, right when the rest of the country was ramping up its holiday frenzy, Douglas's actually shut its doors and shuttered its windows. That's right, it closed during the busiest time of year for buying toys. And during that time, Mr. Douglas

set about creating one-of-a kind, custom toys—
which would be ready just in time for Christmas.

Not once since Mr. Douglas's great-grandfather
started the tradition had the secret of a single toy
made its way into the outside world before Christmas
Eve. But that hadn't kept three generations of
Ravensburg children from wild speculation. In fact,
that was part of the tradition.

Every year on Christmas Eve, the kids of
Ravensburg woke up early and made their way to
Douglas's. As far back as the oldest resident of the town
could remember, at exactly ten o'clock in the morning
the current Mr. Douglas would walk slowly down Main
Street jingling a ring of keys. The children of the town
would follow him, the crowd swelling as he walked
extra slowly toward the long-awaited unveiling.

On this particular Christmas Eve morning, Felix
was only halfway through the left side of the menu
when Stanley noticed it was already 9:55. Time to
get going. He elbowed Felix and nodded toward
Charlotte and Gertie, and they each plunked down
a few dollars before hustling out of the booth and
grabbing their coats from the rack near the door.

As Stanley pulled on his coat, he noticed a large poster on the bulletin board near the front door.

Gertie came up alongside him and read the poster with fake excitement. "Shakespeare on Ice!" she said. "Performed for the entertainment and delight of the good people of Ravensburg by an all-star cast, led by..." Gertie grabbed a black crayon from the front desk and giggled as she drew a mustache on the lead performer. "Led by the stunning Miss Pollyanna Partridge. On December 26th at Lake Ravensburg, at noontide."

Gertie threw her hands in the air. "Noontide? Who says noontide?"

"Polly Partridge?" Stanley said.

Gertie gripped the crayon harder. "And that sort of clever vocabulary deserves a beard, don't you think?"

Stanley turned away and looked around for the others. He spotted Felix blowing kisses toward their booth.

"Thanks for everything, left side. I really do hate to leave you like this," Felix said to what was left of his unfinished breakfast.

Mabel snapped her dishrag at him. "Go join the others, you red-headed garbage disposal. And have fun. And Merry Christmas!"

Stanley held the door open for Charlotte, and the string of bells draped around the handle jingled.

"Thanks," she said.

"No problem. You want to come with us?"

Charlotte looked away, then put her hands into her pockets. "Not this year, okay? I feel like taking a walk."

"Okay. Well, we'll see you back at the treehouse."

Charlotte gave him a sad smile before walking down the street.

Stanley looked back at Gertie, who was dragging Felix away from his meal. Stanley laughed and zipped up his coat.

But the moment his stepped out of the diner and touched Main Street, he was blasted in the face with snowballs.

CHAPTER THREE

THE ULTIMATE SURPRISE

Hoots came from every direction. The English Club was arranged in a fifteen-foot semicircle around a snow-covered Stanley.

"Well, if it isn't widdle Stanley, all covered in snow," said a tall slender girl in the middle of the group.

Gertie stepped up to Stanley's side. "Well, if it isn't Miss Pollyanna Partridge. You look pretty good with short hair, Polly. Although I think you should have left it long... and blue. Blue really was your color."

Polly glared. "Are you talking to me, Short Stuff?"

Gertie showed her teeth. "You and the rest of the grammar police chumps you call friends."

Polly clenched her fists and marched forward. Gertie did the same.

"Right now, Partridge, you and me!" Gertie yelled. "We settle this once and for all. Brilliant, misunderstood, slightly shorter than average sixth grade genius-slash-bombshell, versus the Queen of Bacteria."

Polly clenched her teeth. "Two things, pipsqueak. First, though I may be a genius-slash-bombshell, I am in fact *taller* than average. Secondly, you are not bacteria. You are far worse."

Gertie's face went bright red, and she leapt at Polly.

But out of nowhere a large hand came between them, grabbed Gertie, and pulled her away.

"Ladies, ladies," Felix said. "There are better ways to solve disagreements than with violence. Candy, for one. Eggs Benedict for another. Then there's triple chocolate brownies, peppermint patties, mint chip ice cream... I could go on. So let's smooth things over, shall we? I'll go first. Polly, let me just say that if you *are* the Queen of Bacteria, you are the most attractive bacteria I've ever seen. And, if I may be so bold, any man would be lucky to have such bacteria."

A snowball hit Felix in the side of the head. It was thrown by Gertie. "Whose side are you on, anyway?" she snapped.

"Wait," said Polly, looking at Felix. "Those were supposed to be *compliments*?"

Now Felix was the one to go red in the face. He stuffed his hands in his pockets and swallowed so hard Stanley could see the lump travel down his throat. "Can't we all just get along?" he whimpered.

Just then a rumble went through the crowd. Mr. Douglas had just stepped onto Main Street and was walking toward his toy store.

Stanley turned to face his enemy. "Seriously, Polly," he said. "Can't you give it a rest during the Christmas season?"

Polly shrugged and cackled. Then she held out her arms dramatically and said:

At Christmas I no more desire a rose
Than wish a snow in May's new-fangled mirth
But like of each thing that in season grows...
And, Stanley, 'tis always the season for war.

The English Club roared.

"Save the performance for the ice," said Gertie. "And as much as I'd like to rearrange your face right now, Stanley's right. It *is* the Christmas season. Even if you snobs aren't going to take the high road, I for one will not be brought down to your level. So Merry Christmas, English Club. And may you all get the coal you so richly deserve."

"Hmm," said Polly. "I *might* let that one get to me, if I did not have the satisfaction of knowing widdle Stanley is trying *not* to let on how cold it is as the wet cold slush runs down the inside of his shirt. Warm Christmas wishes to you too, Math Rejectoids!"

Polly snapped her fingers, and the English kids walked away howling.

"You know, Gertie," said Felix. "Sometimes I think you might be right about her."

"You mean that she's a no-good, evil, zombie-like creature from the bottom of a swamp?"

"No," said Felix. "That she looked great with blue hair."

Gertie screamed a ferociously hideous yet completely

silent scream. She ripped at her hair with both hands, then wheeled around and walked away.

Felix shrugged. "Was it something I said?"

"You okay, Stanley?" said a concerned voice.

Stanley turned. It was Charlotte.

"You came back?" Stanley said.

"I thought you guys might need some help with the Creep Squad," Charlotte explained. "But looks like I missed the fun."

Just then the crowd around them exploded into cheers. Mr. Douglas had arrived at his door and had turned to face the crowd. He was holding his keys in the air, jangling them, and the kids of the town were going crazy.

The excitement was electric, and Stanley completely forgot about Polly and the wet slush running down his shirt. Because to Stanley—and every other kid who had ever walked through the doors of that old brick building—there really was nothing quite like Mr. Douglas's toys. They were a combination of old-time wooden craftsmanship and new-age electronic technology that created an end product that was altogether unique.

Stanley remembered the set of Lincoln Logs he'd gotten from Mr. Douglas's when he was little. They could be made into the usual log cabins, but if you snapped them together just right, you could also build a remote-controlled wooden robot. And then there was the football his dad bought him the following year. It looked like any normal foam football—until it hit water. Then it sank to the bottom of the pool and shot back out like a missile.

Stanley knew that Mr. Douglas built these unique toys using incredible craftsmanship and sound science. But still, there was something about them that seemed... magical.

And what made them even more magical was that Mr. Douglas's toys weren't *just* for the children gathered around him that morning. Every year, the master craftsman made a toy for every child in the Ravensburg hospital, and in another longstanding Douglas tradition, he delivered those toys on Christmas Eve night, free of charge.

"Well, children," Mr. Douglas said in his deep, calming voice. "I finished my very last toy at six o'clock this morning, then locked up my shop and went home for a bit to eat and rest." He yawned. "And if you'd allow me, I would love to go home and get some *more* rest right now."

"*Nooo!*" shouted Stanley and the rest of the children, just as they did every year when Mr. Douglas teased them.

He responded with a big belly laugh. "Okay, okay. I suppose I *could* open the door."

"*Yesssss!*" shouted the children, even louder this time.

Mr. Douglas laughed again and turned to the

door. He put a large metal key in the slot, wiggled it around like he didn't know how to work it, and dropped the key ring on the ground. Just like he did every year. And just like *they* did every year, Stanley, his friends, and the rest of the children groaned. The waiting was unbearable.

Mr. Douglas picked up his keys, inserted the biggest one back into the lock, and turned it twice. He looked back at the crowd with a twinkle in his eye. "I hope you enjoy!"

Then he pushed open the door with one arm, and the children pushed under his other arm and into the store.

Stanley could hear the shouts and screams from those who went in first, and he thought to himself that Mr. Douglas must have outdone himself this year. *Maybe he really* does *have a Kid-A-Pult in there.*

As Stanley passed by Mr. Douglas on his way into the store, he told him thank you. And as Mr. Douglas always did, he responded, "You're quite welcome, Stanley."

But as Stanley pushed into the shop, he realized

what the screams and shouts were *really* for. They weren't screams of excitement. They were screams of horror.

Douglas's Toy Store was empty.

Completely bare.

Not one magical toy in the whole magical place.

Stanley turned around to see if this was some kind of prank. But when he saw Mr. Douglas enter the store behind him, he knew immediately this was no prank.

Because Mr. Douglas took one look around, then dropped his keys to the floor, threw his hands to the sides of his head, and screamed.

CHAPTER FOUR

A CALL FOR BACKUP

Police Chief Abrams declared Douglas's Toy Store a crime scene, and within fifteen minutes yellow police tape separated the store from the huge crowd of children gathered on the street waiting for answers.

Some children cried. Others looked angry. But all Stanley could do was watch poor Mr. Douglas. Leaning against the hood of Officer Bobby Evans's police cruiser, the old toymaker looked completely stunned. Stanley couldn't help but think that Mr. Douglas had just lost part of himself. In a way, he probably had.

As the police department's crime crew bustled in and out of the store searching for evidence, most of the children eventually walked away. But not

Stanley and his friends. They walked toward Mr. Douglas.

"Do you have any idea who could have left that note?" Chief Abrams was asking the toymaker.

Mr. Douglas shook his head. "No, sir."

"And you didn't see or hear anything suspicious when you locked up this morning?"

"Nothing. It had just started to snow a little, the street lamps were on, and the whole town was still asleep," Mr. Douglas said. "It was beautiful. I never would have believed that... Why would someone..." He shook his head. "And all the kids! And the little ones in the hospital! Chief, you *have* to find those toys!"

"We're going to do everything humanly possible to track down the thieves, Mr. Douglas. I promise you that."

The chief pulled his radio from his shoulder and held the button down. "This is Chief Abrams, listen up. As of this moment I want every police officer on duty to focus their entire efforts on finding the stolen toys. All exceptions have to be cleared with me. Ladies and gentlemen, you are Ravensburg's finest. If you don't find who did this, no one will. I know you're all as upset about this senseless crime as I am. I'm not going home until I find these guys, and I know I can count on each one of you to give it your all, too."

A series of affirmatives came through the radio. A breach of usual protocol, Stanley suspected, but this was no ordinary crime.

Abrams reattached his radio. "'We've wrapped things up here. But we'll keep you informed, Mr. Douglas. Now I suggest you head home and get some rest."

The chief noticed Stanley and his friends for the first time. He growled. "Not today, kids. I'm in no mood to play math games. In fact, I'm in no decent mood at all. Just stay out of my way and let me do my job." He walked past them, and the look on his face kept Stanley and his friends from saying a word.

Just then, Officer Bobby Evans came out of the toy store. Stanley, Charlotte, Gertie and Felix had helped Evans with two cases in the previous months. Their work had given them and their club, the Math Inspectors, a name around town as amateur detectives.

"Officer Evans, any idea what happened?" Stanley asked.

Evans shook his head. "I can't understand why someone would do this. And on Christmas Eve! Just horrible."

"Any clues in there?" asked Charlotte.

"Just one."

"The note?" Gertie asked.

Evans looked at her quizzically.

"We heard the chief ask Mr. Douglas if he had any idea who would have left a note," Stanley explained. "What did it say?"

The young officer looked thoughtful. "Whoever did this was good. The lab techs have been over every inch of the place. Our thieves must have wiped the place down. No fingerprints, not even from Mr. Douglas. No boot prints. No tire tracks. Nothing except this."

He held out a clear plastic sheath. Inside was a white piece of paper with writing on it.

Stanley grabbed it, and his friends gathered around as he read it aloud.

Merry Christmas! The Grinch

"You're kidding me," said Gertie.

Evans kicked the ground with his boot. "Makes my blood boil."

Stanley looked at him closely. "Everything okay? This one's really shaking you up."

Evans bit his lip. "Timmy, our three-year-old, went into the hospital a few weeks ago. He's getting better—at least, we *think* he's getting better. Doctors say he'll still be in the hospital for another month. Spending Christmas in the hospital is no fun, but—at least he was excited to get one of Douglas's amazing toys." He kicked at the ground. "This *Grinch* stole that from him."

Stanley and Charlotte exchanged a look.

"But there's still hope, isn't there?" Charlotte asked quietly.

"Hope? Today is Christmas Eve, and other than this letter we don't have a clue to go on."

Evans's cell phone rang. He stepped aside to answer it.

"We have to get inside that building, Stanley,"

Charlotte said. "We have to find these punks."

Just then Stanley found himself surrounded by the English Club for the second time that day.

"Not now, Polly, can't you see—"

"Can it," said Polly. "And call off your guard dog." She pointed at Gertie, who indeed was already showing her teeth. "I heard everything the police just said." She put a finger in Stanley's chest. "You wanted a Christmas truce? Well, now you have one. You find the jerks that did this, and you find them fast. You will not get any interference from us." She snapped her fingers, and her friends followed her down the street. She looked back over her shoulder. "At least... not today."

"Well, that was... weird," said Stanley.

He turned to his friends. Gertie and Felix both had their mouths open in surprise. But Charlotte was still staring at the toy store, as if she hadn't even noticed Polly's arrival.

Evans got off his phone. "All right, kids. I'm heading back to the station to do some research on this case. You should probably head on home."

"You have to let us in that building," Charlotte blurted out.

Stanley was about to add his own pleadings, but before he could say a word, Evans lifted up the police tape.

"I was hoping you'd ask," the officer said.

"Really? But... what about Chief Abrams?" Felix said.

"Today I don't care much what Chief Abrams wants," Evans said. "My son is stuck in that hospital bed, and I want to find the sickos who are trying to ruin what little is left of his Christmas. So frankly, I'd appreciate all the help I can get. Everyone has cleared out anyway. Who knows, maybe you'll see something we've missed."

But he didn't sound very hopeful.

As Gertie, Felix, and Charlotte went inside, Evans grabbed Stanley by the forearm. "Please, Stanley," he said. "If there's anything you can do..."

Stanley didn't know what to say, so he just nodded.

Evans walked sadly to his squad car and drove off.

Stanley joined the others inside. Immediately he delegated tasks suited to their strengths. "Charlotte, start snapping mental pictures of this entire place. Gertie, notepad out and ask all the neighbors if they saw or heard anything. Felix, take measurements."

"Of what?"

Stanley threw up his hands. "You guys always ask me that. Of *everything*. Size of exits, estimated amount of toys. What it would have taken to carry them all away. Would they have needed one truck, two trucks? That kind of thing. When you're all done, take out your phones and start searching."

"For what?" Gertie asked.

Stanley glared at her. "Now you're just trying to annoy me."

"It's working, isn't it?"

Stanley shook his head. "You'll be searching for whether this kind of crime ever been committed before. Has this Grinch character ever cropped up before? This side of Whoville, I mean. And where could someone possibly sell those toys?"

The Math Inspectors went to work at a furious pace. The four friends combed through the empty store, taking mental pictures, writing things down, and taking measurements of everything. And then there was the analysis. Or, as Felix liked to call it, *Stanalysis*. Even so, after twenty minutes of observing, measuring, and Stanalyzing, they were no closer to solving the mystery of the lost toys than when they started.

Felix checked his watch. "Bad news, Stanley. An hour and twenty minutes until noontide."

Stanley sighed. "Ten forty. Mr. Douglas makes his hospital delivery around six p.m. We have less than eight hours to find those toys."

"But we don't have a single piece of evidence other than the note," said Gertie. "It's like this crime was committed by a ghost."

Stanley half-expected Gertie to make a spooky sound, but suddenly a thought occurred to him. He reached into his pocket and pulled out his phone. "You might just be on to something, Gertie. About the ghost, that is."

Felix, Gertie, and Charlotte all exchanged a look.

Gertie squinted at Stanley. "You don't mean—"

"Herman?" Stanley answered. "Yeah, I do."

Two months before, the Math Inspectors had been on the trail of a serial vandal who called himself "Mr. Jekyll." After nearly going to jail for the crimes themselves, the friends ended up clearing their names with the help of a new kid at school named Herman Dale. They told Herman that he could start hanging around with them. But so far, that hadn't exactly happened.

"You think Herman did this?" Gertie asked.

"No, I don't," Stanley answered. "But you're right, there's so little evidence, it *is* like a ghost did it.

Herman's the closest thing to a ghost any of us knows. Maybe he could help us."

Gertie looked skeptical. "He's a little weird."

Felix shivered. "I actually have nightmares about him."

"I had forgotten what his name was," said Charlotte.

"No you didn't," said Stanley. "You've got a photographic memory."

"Fine," she said. "I *wanted* to forget his name. The kid gives me the creeps."

Stanley flipped open his cell phone. "We *did* say he could start hanging out with us, didn't we? Well, now's as good a time as any."

"Fine," said Gertie.

"Yeah, okay," said Charlotte.

Felix groaned. "If I wake up one night and my candy stash has been pilfered, you'll all know who to look for."

Charlotte smiled. "A pack of specially trained ninja squirrels?"

Felix's face went white. "Why you gotta go there? What happened to the Christmas season and taking the high road? And not bringing up squirrels?"

"Oh, Felix, 'tis always the season for squirrels," Gertie said.

Stanley texted Herman, and ten minutes later, the small boy was standing in the middle of the spookily empty toy store taking a look for himself.

Herman walked around slowly. He bent down and put his ear to the floor. He smelled the walls. He spun around. Finally he put his hands in his pockets and settled his eyes on the Math Inspectors.

"Haven't heard from you guys in a while," he said.

Stanley looked nervously at Charlotte. "Yeah, well, sorry about that."

Herman twisted his mouth. "You guys still don't trust me, do you?"

Stanley shook his head. "No, Herman, it's not like that at all—"

"And now you need my help," Herman said, almost like an accusation.

Things got uncomfortable, but then Charlotte stepped forward. "Yeah, Herman, you're right. We don't trust you. Maybe you don't remember, but you've done some pretty untrustworthy things. And despite all that, right now, we need your help."

Herman looked at the floor and dug his hands farther into his pockets.

Charlotte moved closer. "How about this: if you don't want to help *us*, that's fine. But what about all the kids in the hospital who aren't going to get one of Douglas's toys this year? How about you help *them*?"

Herman let out a long breath, then pointed to a small window on the second floor that was blacked out with paint. "If the lock wasn't picked, and there was no sign of forced entry on the front or back doors, then your thieves probably came through that window up there."

"That little tiny window?" Stanley said.

"No way," added Charlotte.

"You sure?" said Herman. "It's the most likely entry point to be unlocked, and it's probably easy to pick. It's where *I* would go."

All at once Stanley realized that, since it was blacked out anyway, that window was the only one in the whole building that hadn't been boarded up. "Show me," he said.

CHAPTER FIVE

HIDEOUS ODORS AND DEAD ENDS

Herman led the Math Inspectors out the back door and along the back of the building to a downspout. He wrapped his hands and feet around it and started to shinny up with surprising speed. In less than a minute he was twenty feet up, and he leaned out to grab a thin brick ledge that ran horizontally along the length of the building. His grip was like iron. Holding the ledge with both hands, his legs dangling, he moved along about fifteen feet to the small, blacked-out window.

Herman reached up and gently pushed against the glass with his palm.

The window swung open.

Grabbing the bottom of the windowsill with both hands, he pulled himself through the window and into the building. After a moment, he stuck his head back out.

"See? Easy peasy."

"Herman, that was craze-amazing," Gertie said.

"Insane," agreed Charlotte. "And I know a thing or two about climbing."

"Agreed," said Felix, "and *I* know a thing or two about Chocolate Bacon Bit Cupcakes."

"And what does that have to do with Herman scaling the building like Spider-Man?" Gertie asked.

Felix shrugged. "Beats me. I just thought we were listing things we knew something about." He held up his fingers. "I also know a thing or two about bad breath, foot odor, and stale milk." He scratched his chin. "Come to think of it, that all falls under the subject of hideous odors, so let's just go with that. I know a thing or two about hideous odors."

"Yes," said Gertie. "We know."

By the time the Math Inspectors walked back inside, Herman had already descended the stairs to the main floor. He handed Stanley a piece of paper.

"This fell to the ground when I opened up the window. Must have been placed there by the thieves."

"What makes you think it was the thieves?" Charlotte asked.

Stanley tapped the piece of paper. "Because it's from the book *How The Grinch Stole Christmas*." He turned it toward them, and Gertie read it aloud.

I MUST stop this Christmas from coming!...But HOW?

"So this criminal thinks this is funny?" Charlotte said. "He thinks stealing toys away from kids in the hospital is some kind of *game*?"

"I'm going to be sick," said Gertie. "And then I'm going to hurt someone." She punched Felix.

"Ouch!" he yelled. "What was *that* for?"

"You're someone."

"Can't argue with that," said Felix, rubbing his shoulder. "Stanley, what's that on the back?"

Stanley flipped the paper over. Sure enough, something else had been scrawled on the back. He held it up.

You Stink At Tracking

"What's that supposed to mean?" Charlotte asked.

"I don't know," said Stanley. "But let's go over what we *do* know. With the amount of time it would take to clear out this whole place, there had to have been a whole group of thieves. At least one of them came through that window—he probably let his partners in through the back door. They picked up all the toys and hauled them out of here. And even though they went through the trouble of meticulously wiping the whole place down, they left two paper clues. Why?"

Charlotte growled. "This guy's cocky. Think about it: he calls himself 'the Grinch.' This is probably some sick game to him, and he's willing to throw a few clues our way because he probably doesn't think we can figure them out."

Gertie shook her head. "Well, he's got me stumped. There are *no* footprints outside, and *no* tire tracks of any kind. How'd they pull this off? With the world's quietest helicopter?"

Felix snapped his fingers. "The Kid-A-Pult!"

Gertie rolled her eyes.

"I think I've got it!" Herman said.

Stanley and the others eyed him carefully.

"Well, part of it, at least. It was the word 'stink' in the note. I think *that's* the only part of the clue that is *actually* a clue."

Felix pointed at himself with his thumb. "Wait. Are you saying the thieves are setting *me* up for this whole crime because I'm the expert around here on hideous odors? Well that's just ridiculous. I might stink more than a little on occasion, but that doesn't mean I'm some violent—"

"Zip it, Felix," said Herman. "The note's not talking about you. I think it's talking about something *else* that stinks. Something any professional thief would know all about." He smiled. "Follow me."

Felix looked at Gertie. "Did the new kid just tell me to zip it?"

Gertie smiled. "Yeah. Isn't it awesome?"

Herman led them around the main floor till he located a flight of stairs going down into a cellar. He took it down, then walked slowly around, staring at the concrete floor.

"What are we looking for?" Stanley asked.

"This." Herman put his fingertips into several holes in the ground. He looked around, found something not far away, and brought it back. It was a long screwdriver. He dug it into one of the holes and started to bear down.

A metal disk started lifting off the floor.

Stanley recognized what it was. "A manhole!"

Herman got under the lid with both hands and pushed up until he flipped the manhole cover over. It landed against the floor with a loud slam. He pulled a small flashlight from his pocket and clicked it on.

"Yeah, a manhole. And down there's the sewer. Best way to travel without being spotted."

"You're kidding me," Gertie said, holding her nose.

Herman shook his head. "You '*stink*' at tracking. What else could it mean?"

"No," said Gertie. "I was talking about Felix."

Felix was holding his foot to his nose, sniffing it like a piece of food.

"What? I'm doing a little insta-experiment," Felix explained. "Sometimes my mom tells me my feet smell like a sewer. I wanted to know if she's right."

Herman got on his knees and stuck his head down the manhole for a better look. "Ravensburg has an extraordinary sewer system. Goes everywhere. Larger than necessary—like whoever built the town expected it to become a lot bigger. Also, the rats don't bite much."

Felix stepped toward the hole and looked down. "Okay, two things. First thing, insta-experiment confirms that my feet do *not* in fact smell as bad as a sewer. Big relief there. Second thing, I believe I heard you say something about rats? My guess is you're hiding the fact that there are also squirrels down there, just to give us all a false sense of security. Well, it's not going to work. Therefore, third thing, it's time to call Chief Abrams and bring the professionals in."

Herman pulled his head out of the manhole and gave Felix a funny look. "You don't like squirrels?"

Felix glared. "Don't tell me you're one of those squirrel-loving types."

"Isn't everyone?"

Felix shook his head. "And I thought I knew you."

Herman tossed an extra flashlight to Stanley. "Maybe *you* can convince Mr. Scaredy Pants to come."

"Man up, Felix," said Stanley. "Evans asked us to take a look, and that's what we're doing. Plus, Chief Abrams would sooner shut us down than see us solve another crime. I've learned my lesson: find hard evidence first, tell Abrams second. Simple math."

Charlotte shook her head. "But we have no idea if this is the right way. Maybe the clue meant something else... or maybe it wasn't even a clue."

"Well, we won't know till we take a look down there," Stanley said.

The kids stared at the black hole in the ground. It looked bottomless, smelled stinky, and felt cold.

Stanley gulped. "Listen, nobody's more afraid of dark, creepy places than me. So if *I* can do this, Felix Dervish, Squirrel Enemy Number One can do this too. And so can the rest of you."

Felix threw up his hands in defeat.

Herman put his flashlight in his mouth, climbed into the hole, and slid down the ladder like a fireman. He landed in ankle-deep water and pointed the beam of his flashlight down the tunnel in both directions.

Charlotte went down next, followed by Gertie. That left Felix, who was already sweating like crazy.

"You know," said Stanley, "normally *I'm* the one freaked out about spooky places."

"It's not the sewers," said Felix as he tugged at the

collar of his shirt like he was trying to get more air. "I'm telling you, where there are rats, there are squirrels, Stanley. *Squirrels!*"

Stanley shoved Felix toward the manhole. "That makes zero sense."

"No," whimpered Felix as he climbed down the ladder. "What makes zero sense is the human race's unwillingness to see those fluffy-tailed rodents for the nightmarish creatures they really are."

Stanley was the last to descend the latter. And when he made it to the bottom, the stench of the sewer hit him—hard. Gertie was plugging her nose, and Felix kept lifting his feet out of the water out of fear he was getting bitten. Herman and Charlotte were discussing something.

"So... which way do we go?" Stanley asked.

"That's what we were talking about," said Charlotte. "With this water there's no way of knowing for sure. No footprints or other signs to follow. We're just gonna have to guess."

Stanley thought about it for a moment. "Herman, you're the only one who knows anything about the sewer system. You choose."

Herman pointed his flashlight east. "It's closer to the edge of town this way. That's where I'd head."

No one disagreed, so they set off in that direction.

"Stay close, guys," Herman's voice echoed. "It's harder for the alligators to pick you off if you stay together as a group."

"Alligators?" Felix squeaked.

"I knew there were alligators under this building!" Gertie said.

Herman laughed. "I'm just messing with you.

There are no alligators. See how much fun I am to have around?"

Stanley heard Gertie growl low in her throat.

Every now and then, the sewer tunnel branched off, but Herman never hesitated to lead them straight on.

"How do you know which way to go?" Stanley asked.

"No other choice," Herman called back. "All the side tunnels are dry and don't have footprints. So we follow the main one with water in it until something changes."

"Lucky us," said Gertie. "How much longer will we keep going?"

"However long the trail leads us," Herman replied. "This sewer system is incredible. Goes on forever."

It sure *felt* like it went on forever. For another fifteen minutes they followed the main tunnel as quickly as they could. They were making good time, but the water hid any clues, and they didn't see a single trace of disturbance down any of the side tunnels.

Suddenly, Charlotte shouted. She and Herman had gotten pretty far ahead of the others.

Felix looked spooked. "What did she say?"

Stanley shrugged. "I couldn't make it out through the echoes. Let's go see."

The three stragglers hustled to catch up with Herman and Charlotte. At first it was hard to make out anything in the darkness. Then they all saw it.

A solid wall.

"A dead end!" Gertie squealed. "Great. That means we went the wrong way. We'll have wasted almost an hour by the time we retrace our steps."

Herman made a face. "My bad, guys."

Charlotte started heading back the way they came. "Then let's double-time it and get back as fast as possible."

"Wait—stop," said Felix. "Quiet. Did you hear that? Did it... did it sound like a giant pack of small feet to you?" His voise began to rise in pitch. "I'm calling the cops—before we all die."

"Nobody's going to die," said Stanley calmly. "Let's think for a minute. Herman, is there—"

Herman flashed his light down the side tunnel to

their right. "Wait a second, guys. What in the world...?"

Then Herman sprinted away.

CHAPTER SIX

PATHS IN THE SNOW

Charlotte sprinted after Herman, but Felix screamed and tried to bolt back down the tunnel they way they had come.

Stanley caught him by the arm. "Wait, Felix," he said. "Let's follow them. It can't be that bad if they're running toward it."

"Not true," said Felix. "Maybe Herman and Charlotte secretly work for the squirrels and they're leading us to their nest."

"I was hoping it wouldn't come to this," Gertie said. She reached into her pocket. "Stanley, hold Felix still."

Stanley got behind Felix and pinned his arms. Then Gertie unwrapped a king size candy bar and shoved the whole thing into Felix's impossibly large mouth.

Within seconds, he was a new man.

"Thanks, Gertie," he said. "I needed that. Bravery tank officially refueled. Just point me toward the danger, and stand back!"

Gertie pointed, and Felix took off like a shot.

"Quick thinking," Stanley said.

Gertie shrugged. "Someone's gotta take care of the big lug. Come on, let's catch up."

They found Felix with Herman and Charlotte in the side tunnel, examining something on the floor. This tunnel was even darker than the main one, and it took a minute for Stanley to make anything out in the narrow beam of Herman's flashlight. But soon shapes started to appear.

Wheels. Metal sides. Handles.

"Wagons?" Stanley said.

"Yep," said Herman. "Wagons. Six of them. Small enough to fit inside the tunnels, large enough to carry a good amount of cargo. When I saw tracks and footprints down this tunnel, I knew something was up. There aren't any footprints beyond this point, though."

"Well, great," said Gertie. "Empty wagons. So we

know how they got the toys this far, but what then? They unloaded the toys here. And then... where'd they go?"

Herman started back toward the main tunnel. Curious, the others followed. Herman pointed his light at the ceiling as he walked. When he reached the dead end where they had stopped before, he said, "There! I didn't think to look because there was no ladder. But the ladder's been pulled up."

"What are you talking about?" Stanley asked. He was having trouble making anything out in the darkness.

"I mean the thieves went up. There's a manhole cover up there. And now *we* go up. If we can find a way to get up there."

Charlotte looked up at the manhole cover, then back at the wagons. "Guys, I have a question. How'd they get these wagons down here? I mean, I know that people managed to stick big model ships into tiny bottles, but this is ridiculous."

Felix had wheeled one of the wagons behind him. He ran his hand along it. "You were on to something with the model ships. It looks like the sides of this wagon fold down. My guess is that would make it small enough to fit through the manhole."

Herman nodded. "Probably the only way. Which means they built these wagons *specifically* for this job. Wow. Whoever did this, they've been preparing for it for a while."

"All this for a bunch of toys?" Stanley said. "I just don't get it."

"They *are* the greatest toys in the world," Gertie said. She was holding her nose again, which made her voice sound a bit like a chipmunk's.

Stanley shook his head. "To *kids*, they're the best toys in the world. But to professional thieves? It doesn't add up. Not to me."

"Well," said Herman, "wish me luck." He was already climbing up the wall. Apparently he had found some small cracks that he could use as holds. The kid really was an amazing climber.

But when he reached the top of the wall, the bottom of the ladder was still a few feet away. Herman looked like he was going to try for it, then hesitated.

"Shoot," he said. "I can't reach it." He let out a

groan, climbed back down, and hopped the last five feet to the ground.

Charlotte didn't say a word, but Stanley could see a trace of a smile on her lips. She found the same cracks in the wall, dug in, and climbed. Even though Charlotte was dressed in her usual cutting-edge style, she always chose function over fashion in footwear, and today, her all-terrain boots made quick work of the sewer walls.

When she got to the same spot Herman did, she didn't stop. Instead, she grunted... and leapt. She flew through the air and grabbed onto the lowest rung of the ladder with her right hand.

The ladder came down immediately, and Charlotte with it. But just before it hit, Charlotte dove, rolled, and gracefully bounced up to her feet.

Herman's mouth dropped open. "Um, that was... pretty good. And I know a thing or two about climbing."

Charlotte looked at Stanley and winked.

"Wait, are we talking about the things we know about again?" Felix asked. "Because in addition to hideous odors, I'm also quite knowledgeable about a number of high-calorie dessert items."

Gertie groaned. "We know, Felix."

Herman climbed the ladder and put his head against the manhole cover, which Stanley now saw was slightly ajar. Herman pressed his hands and his head against the cover and pushed the metal plate up and over. Then he squeezed through. The rest of the kids climbed up and joined him.

Once again, Stanley took the ladder last. To his surprise, he didn't exit onto a street, but into a grove of trees thick enough to shroud them in a blanket of semi-darkness. The manhole was situated right in the dirt near the top of a sloping hill.

He looked down the hill and saw his friends at the bottom.

"Down here," said Charlotte. "They went north, toward the river."

As Stanley joined his friends, he saw what had led them that direction. Since the trees were thick around the manhole, there was very little snow. But cut into the dirty slush, two broad paths ran north down the face of the hill. As if two large things had been dragged. Big things. Heavy things.

Like maybe large bags of toys.

"This way." Charlotte pointed toward the muffled sound of running water.

Stanley squinted and saw the paths grow more distinct as the trees thinned out and the snow grew deeper.

The kids set out at once. Soon the late December sun began to reflect off the growing patches of snow, and it didn't take long for Charlotte and Herman to speed ahead, as they had before.

Stanley turned around to the others. "Hurry up, you guys. Herman and Charlotte are already out of the woods."

Gertie didn't look like she was planning on quickening her pace. Neither did Felix.

"Fine," Stanley said. "I'm going to catch up. You two just follow our tracks."

He sprinted toward the tree line, taking the last three steps at a leaping pace. And all at once, two things happened.

He was free of the woods.

And he was hit hard in the chest.

Stanley collapsed to the ground, struggling to breathe. He looked up.

Herman stood over him.

"Why?" Stanley gasped.

But Herman just smiled.

CHAPTER SEVEN

WE GOT THEM!

"Why?" asked Stanley again.

Herman pointed.

A few feet away, Charlotte stood looking over the edge of a cliff. A few rocks at her feet slid over the side and plunged into a river far below. If Stanley hadn't stopped when he did, he would have run right off that cliff.

Stanley gulped, then offered Herman a weak smile. "Thank you."

"No problem," said Herman. "But I'm sorry to say, we've lost the trail."

"Where?" asked Gertie, who had just arrived with Felix.

"Right over the edge of this cliff," said Herman.

The friends stood looking into the water below.

"I don't get it," Charlotte said. "You think they threw the toys into the river?"

"No way," said Stanley. "Why steal the toys only to destroy them?"

Felix scratched his cheek. "Solved it, everybody. See that large group of sticks right there?" He pointed to a spot on the shore where branches were piled up. "That's right, ladies and gentlemen, our elusive Grinch is nothing more than a family of beavers. What else explains the trail going cold right here?"

Gertie sighed and shook her head. "You want a better explanation? How about humanoid *non*-beavers lowering bags of toys onto a boat and taking off down the Minuit River?"

Felix rubbed Gertie's head with his hand. "Gertie, Gertie. My adorable, naïve little Gertie. Beavers may not be quite as bad as squirrels, but they are certainly part of the small, furry domination of our planet. If you think for one minute—"

"Felix!" growled Charlotte. "Shut it."

"Yes, ma'am," Felix whimpered.

Charlotte pointed down. "So. They drag the toys

to the cliff, lower them down to a boat below, and off they go?"

Stanley nodded. "Appears so. And I don't see any boats on the water."

"So they've obviously got the jump on us. But how much? That's the question."

Herman smiled. "Not to be overdramatic, but it sounds to me like this is a job for... *da da da da*! The *Math Inspectors*!"

"Point taken," said Stanley. "Let's run it through."

"Run it through?" Herman asked.

"Oh, yeah, sorry. It's something we say when we're going to talk about a problem out loud. Especially when there's numbers involved."

"So why don't you just say, 'Let's talk about the problem out loud'?"

"Because 'let's run it through' is less words," Stanley said.

Herman smiled. "See how much I'm already learning about math?"

"'Run it through' is also way cooler," Felix added. "And speaking of cool, want me to show you our Math Inspectors call-to-action moves? I'm the multiplication sign—"

"Maybe some other time, Felix," Herman said.

"Yeah," agreed Gertie. "Maybe when we're not so close to a fifty-foot cliff."

"So," Stanley began, "running it through. Mr. Douglas said he left the shop at six a.m. Let's assume the robbers broke in not long after that. How long would it take for them to remove all the toys, wipe the place down, pull the wagons with the toys down the sewer, then drag them over this cliff?"

Herman took off his cap and ran a hand through his hair. "Well, judging by the size of Douglas's, I can guess at the amount of toys, and... I'm gonna say about four hours."

"You're sure?" asked Stanley. "Could it have been two or three?"

Herman shrugged. "I guess, but if you want my expert criminal opinion, I'm giving it. That's an awful lot of toys and a really big job. I'm saying four hours."

Stanley nodded. "Okay then. So the toys were lowered to a boat at ten a.m. How far could they have gotten by now?"

Herman shrugged. "Guess it depends on how fast the boat goes."

"I don't suppose you have some mysterious knowledge of boating on the river that I don't know about?" Stanley asked. "Because that would really come in handy right about now."

"Actually, I do," said Herman.

"Seriously?"

"Yeah. My uncle Farley takes me out all the time."

"Great, so how fast—"

"Hold it, hold it!" said Felix as he held up his hand. "Just wait one beaver-building minute."

"You figured something out?" Gertie asked.

"Only that Herman has an uncle named Farley. Are you kidding me? Stanley, how can you just move on like that after he tells you he's got an uncle named *Farley*?"

"Because we're in the middle of trying to find toys for a bunch of sick kids," Stanley said.

"Oh, come on, his uncle's name is *Farley*! I mean, if you had given me one guess as to what Herman's uncle's name is, my first guess would have been Cooter. My *second* guess would have been Farley."

"Are you making fun of me?" Herman asked.

"Herman, his name is *Farley*! Of *course* I'm making fun of you. Please tell me he fixes tractors, or arm-wrestles for a living, or re-enacts Civil War battles."

Herman rolled his eyes. "If I tell you, will you shut up and help us find these toys?"

"Promise."

"Fine. Uncle Farley traps animals for a living."

Felix threw his hands in the air. "I rest my case. Of course he traps animals for a living."

"And he fishes on the Minuit using a bow and arrow."

"This is even better than I expected."

Herman let out a long breath. "And he raises show chickens."

Felix fell to the ground and started beating his hands into the snow. "He raises *show chickens*! I don't even know what that is, but I think Uncle Farley might be the greatest American alive. Can I meet him someday?"

"Can we find the toys first?" Herman said.

But Felix couldn't even talk, he was laughing so hard.

Herman looked at the others. "And he thinks *I'm* the weird one?"

Charlotte shrugged. "He grows on you."

"Yeah," said Gertie. "Like a fungus you can never get rid of."

"You said you know the river," said Stanley, steering the conversation back to the problem at hand. "What can you tell us?"

"Well," Herman said, "this is the Minuit River, a tributary of the Hudson."

"How far is it before it feeds into the Hudson?"

Charlotte asked.

"About ten miles."

"Is that ten miles as the Farley floats?" Felix asked.

Herman shrugged. "I mean... yes...?"

Felix crossed his lanky arms and looked very satisfied with himself. "So the question is: *How fast could a Farley float if a Farley could float fast?*"

Gertie sighed. "Just pretend he was asking about the speed of boats in general."

Herman ran a hand through his hair and let out a breath. "Wow, well... it depends on a lot of things. It's winter right now, and although the rivers around here almost never freeze over, there's usually enough ice to make travel difficult."

"Usually?" Gertie said.

"Well, this December's been a little warmer than usual." He pointed down to the river. "There's *some* ice, but quite a bit less than normal. See, in summer, with a wide-open river, following the channels correctly? Uncle Farley can get that thing doing thirty-five miles per hour, no problem."

"How about now?" Stanley asked.

Herman looked down at the river again. "I think they'd be lucky to do fourteen."

"Okay," said Stanley, "so fourteen miles per hour. Felix, I need you to stop being Weird Felix and go back to being Brilliant Felix."

Felix popped up straight and threw Stanley a salute. "Using smartphone to find nautical maps of the Hudson River and neighboring tributaries, sir!"

"Gertie," Stanley said, "what's the time?"

Gertie looked at her wrist. "11:22 by my watch."

"So if we're right, and the thieves hit the water at ten o'clock, they've been traveling for one hour and twenty-two minutes. So, at fourteen miles per hour, how far could the boat get in one hour and twenty-two minutes? Could they reach the Hudson?"

"But Stanley," said Charlotte, "we don't even know for sure that they went toward the Hudson. What if they went the other way?"

Herman shook his head. "They headed to the Hudson, all right. The other way gets rough and narrow real quick."

Gertie waved her pen. "I'm with Charlotte. We're making too many assumptions. What if they found a way to go faster, or slower? What if they stopped along the way? There's any number of variables that we don't know."

"Exactly," said Stanley. "Variables we *don't* know. So let's go with what we *do* know, because right now it's all we've got."

"You got a feeling about this one?" Charlotte said.

"Close enough," he said. "Gertie, do some math."

"Okay. If we multiply fourteen miles per hour times 1 hours and 22 minutes, we get..."

"Wait!" said Herman, shaking his head. "That's not right. That's not how it works."

"How *what* works?" Stanley asked.

Herman looked at Stanley and then the others. "You mean *I* know something about math that *you* guys don't?"

Gertie spun her finger as a sign to speed things up. "If you do, now would be a really good time to enlighten us."

"Okay," Herman said. "Uncle Farley taught me long ago that the speed of the boat on the speedometer doesn't usually reflect the *real* speed of the boat on the river."

Stanley slapped his head. "Because of the current!"

Herman pointed at him. "Exactly. Depending on whether you're traveling upstream and against the current, or downstream and with the current, the real speed of the boat will either be *less* than the boat's speedometer speed or *more* than the speedometer speed."

Stanley looked thoughtful. "I see. So we need to *subtract* the speed of the current from the speedometer speed if the boat's going *against* the current, or *add* the speed of the current to the speedometer speed if the boat's going *with* the current."

"Great, so what's the speed of the current?" Gertie asked.

Herman shrugged. "Oh heck, I don't know. I mean, it changes all the time."

Stanley let out a low growl. "Felix, you got something yet?"

"Aye aye, sir. Nautical maps of the Hudson and all corresponding lakes, rivers, tributaries, *and* estuaries."

"Anything about current?"

"Lots of things about current."

"Lots of things about the current right now?"

"You mean *currently*?" Felix said with a grin. "Um, well, it looks complicated."

"Then it's a good thing," said Stanley, "that you're a genius."

"An excellent point, sir. Well, ahh... it looks like, adjusting for... um, I'd say five miles per hour."

"And that could be off by how much?" Gertie asked.

Felix smiled and pointed to his head. "By nothing. Remember the genius thing?"

Stanley turned back to Herman. "One last thing we need to know. Once the boat goes from the Minuit River into the Hudson, would they have traveled north or south?"

"North takes you to Albany, and I suppose they could head that way... but frankly, I'd go south. It's faster going, plus it gets you into heavy population more quickly. Easier to get lost in the crowds."

"So you think they'd be traveling with the current when they reach the Hudson, too," Gertie said.

Herman nodded.

"Got it," said Stanley. "So. We take 14 miles per hour and add to it the 5 miles per hour of the current. That means the real speed of the bad guy boat is 19 miles per hour. Gertie, take it away."

"So, I take 19 and multiply it by..." She looked down at her watch yet again. "1 hour and 25 minutes. And that gives me..."

"Wait!" said Stanley. "Calculate how far they'll have travelled as of five minutes from now. Felix, I'll need you to then translate that into a location on the map."

While he left Gertie and Felix to work out the problem, Stanley took out his phone, pressed speaker, and dialed a familiar number.

"Stanley," Officer Evans said after two rings. "Please tell me you got something, because we've got a whole lot of nothing."

"Maybe, but it will take me too long to explain. You just have to trust me."

"I don't have any other choice. What have you got?"

"We know where the thieves are going to be in five minutes."

There was a pause on the other end of the line. Then Evans said, "Where?"

"They're on a boat on the Hudson."

"The Hudson River?" said a surprised Officer Evans.

"Yes, and in five minutes we think they will be..." Stanley nodded his chin toward Gertie.

"Five minutes from now will be 11:30. That means they'll have been on the river for about 1 hour and 30 minutes. So one and a half hours, or 1.5 hours. I multiply 19 miles per hour by 1.5 hours, and that gives me..."

"28.5 miles," blurted out Felix.

Gertie glared at him. "I seriously hate when you do that."

Stanley pointed at Felix. "Location?"

"Okay," said Felix. "It's 10 miles from this point of the Minuit River until it opens into the Hudson. From there, another 18.5 miles puts them right... there." He stuck his enormous finger on the screen and turned it around so Stanley could see.

"Officer Evans, they'll be a half mile north of Newburgh and Beacon at eleven thirty. You don't happen to know anybody in either of those towns, do you?"

"No, darnit, but I sure wish I—wait a second. *I* don't know anybody, but Chief Abrams... Stanley, I gotta run."

The line went dead.

The kids could hardly breathe as they waited for the phone to ring. Time seemed to slow down. Five minutes passed. Then seven. Finally, the digital ringtone sounded, and Stanley nearly mashed the speakerphone button to pieces in his excitement.

"Did you get them?"

"Stanley, sometimes I think you kids are magicians."

Stanley's eyes grew wide. "You got them?"

"Yes, Stanley, we got them."

CHAPTER EIGHT

TWO MORE PATHS?

Felix and Herman high-fived each other, Charlotte pumped her fist, and Gertie did a little dance.

"We need details," said Stanley. "How'd you do it?"

"It certainly wasn't me," Evans said. "Chief Abrams made a direct call to the cell phone of the chief of police in Beacon, which is where Abrams worked before he came to Ravensburg. Within two minutes of that call, Beacon contacted their patrol boat on the Hudson. Officers boarded the thieves' boat just a couple miles north of where you said it would be."

"Not too bad," Felix said.

"Within a reasonable margin of error, I'd say," Gertie agreed.

"And Stanley," Officer Evans continued, "they found enormous red canvas bags on board. We're talking big bags. *Santa Claus* bags. The bags were chained and padlocked shut, and last I heard they were going to get a pair of bolt cutters—oh... wait a second."

Officer Evans was suddenly gone, and the kids waited impatiently.

A minute later Evans returned. "Stanley," he said. His voice was quiet.

"The toys?" Stanley asked.

"They found toys. Just not *Mr. Douglas's* toys."

"What? What are you talking about?"

"Each bag was packed tight with the same identical green stuffed animal. The officer I spoke to figures there's got to be a couple hundred of them, all identical. Every single one of them."

"What do you mean? There was nothing in the bags but stuffed animals? What stuffed animal?"

"The Grinch, Stanley. The thieves were carrying four bags filled with nothing but Grinch stuffed animals."

Stanley was speechless. He looked at his friends.

"What about the thieves themselves?" Charlotte asked. "Are they talking?"

"There were four men on board," said Evans. "But they're pretty rough-looking characters, and they're not saying a word. You kids did good, but... well, it looks like we're back to square one. Listen, I better get back to work. If you learn anything new... well, you let me know right away."

"Yes, sir, we will," Stanley said before hanging up.

The kids walked silently away from the cliff, back through the woods, and toward the manhole cover that led to the sewers.

"I don't understand," Stanley finally said, breaking the silence. "If that's not where the toys are, where *else* could they be?"

Gertie patted him on the shoulder. "Listen, Stanley, as you've said before, sometimes things are messy. I told you there were a ton of variables we didn't know. What if they stopped the boat, dropped off the real toys somewhere along the way, and then kept going?"

"But our math was right on the nose. We found them. How would they have had the time to do that?"

Gertie shook her head. "Maybe the current was flowing faster than we thought, or their boat went faster than we estimated. It could have been any number of things."

Stanley looked to Charlotte and Herman. They both shrugged. Then he looked at Felix.

"There *are* a lot of maybes here," Felix said.

"Yeah," said Stanley. "That's what I mean. Listen, the math wasn't wrong. The math was right." His eyes suddenly widened. "*Eerily* right."

"Meaning what?" Charlotte asked.

Stanley pushed his glasses up the bridge of his nose. "Meaning we followed them all the way out here and guessed where to find their boat—pretty close to where they actually were. And the only reason we did all that was because they left clues the whole way. I bet they *wanted* us to follow them and come up empty-handed. It was all just a wild goose chase."

"Well," said Gertie, "it worked. The chase is over, and we're clueless. I mean, without clues."

"Unless..." said Charlotte. Suddenly she took off through the woods at a sprint.

"Unless what?" yelled Stanley.

But she didn't answer.

"Charlotte! Unless what?"

The rest of them ran after her.

By the time they caught up, Charlotte was on her knees in the dirty snow on the far side of the manhole cover. She pounded her fists into the ground.

"So stupid," she said. "How could I have not seen them?"

"Seen what?" Stanley said as he came up behind her.

Charlotte pointed. Plain as day, on the back side of the hill, were two sets of paths cut into the sludge, each going in a different direction. "I never saw them. Never even looked. I wasn't even thinking about more than one path, let alone three. I came out of the manhole, saw the one leading down the hill, and I fell for it. Dumb, stupid, me."

"Charlotte," said Herman, "I didn't see them either. None of us did."

"*Three* sets of paths?" Gertie said. "Three directions? What's going on here?"

Stanley punched his own hand. "The real toys were never on that boat. They left three paths for us to find, and we chose the wrong one."

"It's like that game, Three-Card Monte," Herman said. "They have you looking three different directions so you don't know where the card is hidden."

Stanley nodded. "Well, we know the real toys weren't on the boat, so the good news is we've eliminated one of the three paths. Time to see where these other two lead."

He looked at the others. "Felix and Gertie, you

take the path on the right. Charlotte, Herman, and I will take the one on the left. Let's meet back here in ten minutes."

Ten minutes later they were back at the manhole cover comparing notes.

"Our path led to the highway," Felix reported. "From the tire tracks on the shoulder of the road, it looked like a big truck pulled over. It must have been to load the bags, because that's where the drag marks ended."

"Which direction was the truck headed?" Stanley asked.

"West, into the Rondout Valley."

"And our path led east, deeper into the woods," said Charlotte. "The footprints and the drag marks ended at the railroad tracks a couple hundred yards from here."

"I don't supposed you know which direction the train was going," Felix said.

"South," Charlotte answered.

"How do you know?" Felix asked.

"I put my ear against the track."

"That actually works?"

Charlotte laughed. "Nah. It could have been going north. To be honest, I have no idea."

Stanley had heard enough. "All right guys, let's work the problem. I'll call Officer Evans. Felix, can you—"

"Pull up maps of highways and railroads for the area?" Felix said. "Already on it."

"And I've got my pencil out and I'm not afraid to use it," Gertie said.

"I'm ready to pummel the thieves whenever we catch them," Charlotte added.

Herman looked lost. "What about me?" he said. "What's my role here?"

"Um... I'm not exactly sure what you do yet," Stanley said.

Felix looked up from his phone. "He could tell us Uncle Farley stories. I mean, what's Christmas Eve without stories about show chickens and stuffed critters?"

"My uncle would never stuff a critter," Herman said. "The pelts and skins are too valuable."

"Wow," said Felix. "I mean, just wow. Uncle Farley is the gift that keeps on giving."

Shaking his head, Stanley dialed Officer Evans, who picked up right away. This time, Stanley told him everything: about the note, the sewer system and wagons, the drag marks in the snow, and about how they had estimated the location of the boat. Then he told him about the two new paths.

"Do you think you kids can come up with some approximate locations for the thieves?"

"We're working on it," Stanley said. "Give us five minutes."

"That will give me enough time to update the chief."

"Does he know we're helping out yet?" Stanley asked.

"No, but he's about to," Evans said before ending the call.

Stanley flipped his phone shut and turned to Felix. "You got anything on that train?"

"Yeah. If they were going south, the track leads into Pennsylvania. Looks like the speed limit for freight trains on this track is 49 miles per hour. If they found some way to board the train here around 10 a.m., then that means they've been traveling for just about two hours. Two hours multiplied by 49 miles per hour equals 98 miles. Allentown, Pennsylvania is 106 miles from this spot."

"Great work, Felix. But what if they traveled north?"

Felix shook his head. "They didn't. The only train that passed by here this morning was headed south. And it would have been here at around 10 a.m., just like we thought."

"Which brings up the question: how on earth did the thieves board a train that was traveling 49 miles per hour?"

"Horses?" Gertie suggested.

"Kid-A-Pult?" Felix offered.

Charlotte laughed. "The train wasn't moving. My dad and I have been hunting out in this area. The tracks are really old here, so the trains have to stop and wait for the tracks to be manually switched. I bet the thieves knew this."

Stanley took out his phone and dialed Evans again. "Officer Evans, we think the train is heading to Allentown."

"Pennsylvania?"

"Yep."

Evans let out a loud sigh. "Okay then. Looks like the chief has more phone calls to make. And the highway path?"

"Just as soon as we have it." Stanley ended the call and looked at Gertie. "What have you got?"

"Okay," she said, tapping her pencil against her notepad. 'This one is messier. We know they were headed west toward the Rondout Valley, but we have no idea where they went after they got there."

"So give us all the possibilities."

"That's going to be difficult."

"Why?"

Gertie chewed on the end of her pencil. "Well, say they drove the four miles to Highway 209 and then took it north. If they didn't stop, then traveling at 65 miles per hour, they could be in Queensbury by now."

"Great," said Felix. "So we just need to—"

"I'm not finished," said Gertie. "Let's say instead of going all the way north, they crossed the Hudson at Lake Katrine, then drove south. In that case, they could be in New York City, assuming the traffic's not too bad."

Stanley shook his head. "The police would never find them in New York City."

"It gets worse," Gertie said. "If they took Highway 209 South, they could be in New Jersey, or Eastern Pennsylvania. Heck, practically Philly."

Stanley's shoulders slumped. "There's no way we're going to find those toys."

"And I'm not even done," Gertie said. "On the off chance that they decided to take one of those old twisty roads west into the teeth of the Catskill Mountains, well... they could be hiding anywhere."

"In other words, needle in a haystack," Charlotte said.

Gertie shook her head. "Think of it as a needle, in a dumpster of needles, hidden inside a giant haystack."

Stanley dialed Evans and gave him the bad news.

"Okay," said Evans. "We'll just have to call in all the help we can get. The good news is, we *do* have a lot of help. Stealing toys from a bunch of sick kids on Christmas Eve seems to have gotten everybody's attention, and we're getting offers to help by the minute. I've never seen it like this at the station.

Every off-duty police officer in town has shown up without even being asked. Remember, all of them were kids once, too.

"And with this newest information, we'll be able to bring in the Highway Patrol. Several different Highway Patrols. Heck, we've even had security guards and mall cops show up and demand we use them.

"Anyway," Evans finished, "you kids have already done a lot. I think it's time for you to head back into town. There's nothing else to do now but wait."

"I hate waiting," Stanley said.

"I know you do. But Stanley, thank you."

"Well, guys," said Stanley after ending the call, "let's get back to town. It's going to be quite a hike."

"We're walking?" Felix asked. "The highway isn't exactly a straight shot—it'll take us forever. And it's freezing. Couldn't we just call somebody?"

"Waiting for a ride won't save us much time," said Herman. "And there's no need." He walked over to the manhole and pointed down.

Gertie frowned. "Are you serious?"

Herman shrugged. "You want a straight shot?

Herman provides a straight shot."

Gertie plugged her nose. "Well, Gertie's not thrilled. But you're probably right. It *is* the quickest way back."

One by one, the friends took the ladder down into the sewers. As usual, Stanley brought up the rear. As he stepped down, he looked one last time at the paths in the snow, wondering if they would turn up any new leads. Then he sighed, pulled the cover down behind him, and descended into the darkness of the tunnel.

CHAPTER NINE

CHRISTMAS EVE ON MAIN STREET

It was a long quiet walk back through the sewer system, up into the basement of Douglas's Toy Store, and out onto Ravensburg's Main Street. Stanley and his friends were cold and tired, but nobody was quite ready to head home.

Without exchanging a word, they made their way to their usual booth at Mabel's Diner. They ordered sandwiches and introduced Herman to Mabel's famous S'morelicious Hot Chocolate.

After lunch, Mabel wheeled out Felix's unfinished breakfast. "I figured you'd be back for it sometime today," she said as she slid it in front of him. "I just thought it would be under happier circumstances, and..." Her eyes watered, and she blew her nose into her apron. Then she set out strawberry syrup for Felix's hash browns and walked sadly back into the kitchen.

The kids were silent except for the loud slurping of hot chocolate. At one point, through a mouthful of food, Felix said, "I don't suppose anybody wants to revisit the topic of Herman's Uncle Farley, do they?"

Each one of them gave Felix a sour look, and he went back to eating the left side of the menu.

Stanley's phone rang sometime between the side of bacon and the cheddar cheese omelet. He put it on speaker. "Officer Evans?"

"Well, we were able to reach the Allentown Police Department," Evans said. He didn't sound happy.

"And?" Stanley asked.

"They got the train stopped. Stanley, you guys were right again."

"You found the toys?"

"We found four large canvas bags. Each chained and padlocked. When they opened them up, they found hundreds of Grinch stuffed animals."

"Again?" Charlotte said.

"And no thieves this time," Evans continued. "Not even a trace. Allentown PD is making a general search of the area as we speak."

"And that's it?"

"That's it. No sign of the truck. With that large of an area I doubt we'll ever find them, but... I just wanted to give you an update."

Gertie looked like she was about to explode. "Officer Evans, why is somebody going to so much effort to steal toys?"

"I wish I knew, Gertie. This Grinch either really hates sick kids, or these toys are worth a lot more than I ever imagined. Look, guys, the chief told me to go be with my family up at the hospital, but I want to stay involved with the—" He paused. "Kids, hold on a moment."

The friends looked at each other. They could hear shouting in the background on Evans's end of the line.

Evans came back a minute later out of breath. "Kids, I think we may have caught a break! A deputy sheriff over in Shandaken found an abandoned truck just a few minutes ago."

"And let me guess," said Gertie. "They found four large bags of Grinch toys in the back of the truck?"

"No, that's just it. The truck was empty. But there was a ramp leading away from the truck, and four different sets of four-wheeler tracks leading away from the vehicle."

"Where to?"

"North of Shandaken into the heart of the Catskill Mountains. We're calling everybody right now and redirecting the search. In fact, now that I'm thinking about it... we could use your help one last time. I have no idea how far four-wheelers could have gone by now, but if you kids could give us an idea, that would really help with the search."

"Consider it done," said Charlotte. "We'll call you as soon as we know."

Stanley looked around. Felix was already typing away on his tablet, Gertie was busy writing something on her pad, Charlotte was practicing her knockout punch, and Herman was looking awkward.

Stanley grabbed a crayon from the table next to them, flipped over his paper menu, and started to draw:

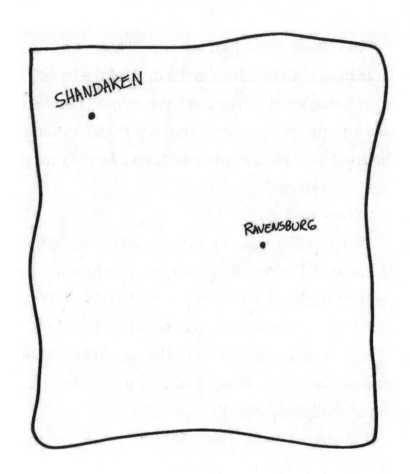

Herman leaned in. "What's that?"

"It's a map of the area around Ravensburg and the Catskills area around Shandaken."

"You call that a map?"

"A *rough* map. As soon as Felix and Gertie have some info I'll start plotting it in."

"But it's just a square with two dots. And a really,

really terrible square at that."

"What's that supposed to mean?" Stanley said.

"It was meant to be an insult," said Herman. "Hence the word terrible."

"You think you could do better?"

Herman flipped over his own menu, reached into his pocket, and pulled out a small canvas bag. He unrolled the bag to reveal several different kinds of pencils. He selected the one in the center, put his pencil to the paper, and began.

"Why does that pencil look different from the ones I have at home?" Stanley asked.

"This is Big Bertha. She's a charcoal pencil," Herman explained.

Stanley watched in amazement as a professional-looking map of Ravensburg and the surrounding region appeared before his eyes within minutes.

"Herman, that's... that's..."

"Pretty good, don't you think?"

"No, Herman, not *pretty* good. That's unbelievable. You're an artist?"

He smiled. "I dabble."

"Okay then, let's put this map to use. Gertie, what have you got?"

Gertie looked up from her pad. "More mess, I'm afraid. It's hard to know how fast these four-wheelers are going. They can go as fast as 50 miles per hour on the highway, but Charlotte thinks they'd be lucky to do much more than 10 miles per hour through the heavy forest they're traveling. So I'm warning you, this is a total guess. We could be way off."

"We have to start somewhere. So go ahead."

"Well, they've been on their ATVs for approximately 4 hours. At 10 miles per hour, they'd have made it about 40 miles."

"What if somebody picked them up?" Stanley asked.

"Then we're out of luck," said Gertie. "But since we have no way of knowing exactly... Here, Herman, hand me that map. What we *do* know is that the four-wheeler tracks ran north from Shandaken. If the thieves traveled northwest, they could be as far as Oneonta by now." Gertie drew an 'X' on that spot. "If they traveled straight north, they could be to Cobleskill by now. And if they went northeast, they'd be really close to Albany."

The Math Inspectors all leaned in and looked at the map while Herman connected the dots between Shandaken, Oneonta, Cobleskill, and Albany.

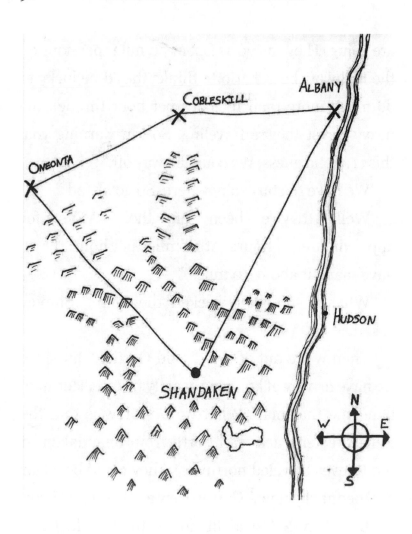

Herman frowned. "That's still a really big area."

Gertie tapped the map with her pen. "With the information we have, it's the best we can do."

Stanley picked up his phone and dialed what had by now become a very familiar number. "Officer

Evans," he said, "we ran the numbers and, well, I sure hope you've got a lot of men."

When Stanley told Evans the three towns that made up the outer limits of the search perimeter, Evans sounded exhausted. "Well, at least we've got every law enforcement resource for three counties helping us out. But I'll be honest, we're gonna need a miracle to find those toys by tonight."

He let out a long, sad sigh. "But you kids shouldn't have your Christmas ruined," he said. "I'm thankful for all you've done, but you need to get home to your families."

There was a moment of silence. Then Evans added: "Merry Christmas, kids."

The call ended, and Stanley and the others just looked at each other with sad faces. *Yeah*, Stanley thought. *A real Merry Christmas.*

As he flipped his phone shut, Mabel arrived at their table, trying to muster a smile.

"Sorry kids, but Christmas calls. We're closing early. The bank, the general store, pretty much all of Main Street is closing at three o'clock today. And I suspect it's time you all ran home and helped your folks get ready for Christmas Eve."

Mabel and Evans were both right. The Math Inspectors had done their best, and now it was up to the search parties. Either the toys would be found, or more likely... they wouldn't. As large as the search area was, the odds were seriously against a happy ending.

The bells on the door rang hollow as the five friends shuffled out onto Main Street. The overcast skies made it seem a lot later than it was. The lampposts had flickered to life, and the holiday lights on the buildings stood bright against the darkening day. Large snowflakes swayed softly to the ground. The city's giant blue spruce, decorated with bright lights, enormous ornaments, and oversized candy canes, stood sparkling in the center of the square. Just like every Christmas Eve.

But one thing was missing. Sound. Not a single Christmas carol came from the businesses on Main Street. And nobody even lifted their eyes toward each other as they moved on their way.

Stanley pulled his hood down over his ears and his coat collar up over his mouth. He looked at his watch. There was just enough time for one important stop.

CHAPTER TEN

CHARLOTTE'S SECRET

When the Math Inspectors arrived at Ravensburg General Hospital, they were greeted by a young nurse sitting at the receptionist's desk.

Stanley's mom worked there, so he knew almost all of the nurses. "Hi, Missy," he said. "Where's Al?"

"Hey, Stanley. Al and the rest of our security guards are trying to help out with the Grinch hunt. They know a lot of the kids who'll be here over Christmas, and they all took the thefts personally. But why are you kids here? You should all be home."

"We wanted to see Timmy Evans," Gertie said.

Missy gave a look of understanding. "Okay, but not too long. He's up on the second floor at the end of the north hall. Stanley, you know the way."

They took the stairs and walked down the

hallway. A large figure came out of one of the rooms and almost ran them over.

"Oh, sorry, Chief Abrams," said Stanley, jumping to the side.

The chief's eyes opened wide, and then his face scrunched up so much it looked like his mustache had taken over the lower part of his head. "You kids are everywhere I step some days," he barked.

"Now, Harry," said a woman's voice just inside the room. "You aren't exactly lightening the mood around here."

A tall pretty woman followed Abrams into the hallway and shut the door behind her. She looked to be in her late forties, maybe fifty, and her brown hair was pulled back into a tight ponytail. "Will you introduce me?" she said.

The chief rolled his eyes but turned to the kids and said, "This is my wife, Lizzie. And Lizzie, these four here call themselves 'The Math Inspectors.'" He pointed at Herman. "I have idea who that one is. Don't tell me you're multiplying?"

"His name is Herman Dale," said Charlotte. "And he's the main reason you have any lead on the Grinch."

Mrs. Abrams broke into a huge smile. "Oh, *now* I know who you are. You are the clever kids who helped my Harry crack the Claymore Diamond case. Do you mean to tell me you were the ones who tracked the thieves this morning from Douglas's Toy Store? However did you do such a thing?"

"Don't encourage them, Lizzie. Their heads are already big enough. Enough chit-chat and touchy feely stuff. I need to—"

The chief's cell phone rang, and he stepped aside.

Mrs. Abrams looked conspiratorially at the kids and whispered, "*Now* do you want to tell me how you followed the Grinch?"

"It was Herman who found the clue," said Stanley. "It was a note from the Grinch."

Gertie patted Herman on the shoulder. "He also knew that the thieves' message on the back was inviting us to follow them on a scenic tour of the sewer systems. But I forgive him, because it worked."

"I see," said Mrs. Abrams. "Well, it seems we owe you all a debt of gratitude."

"Fine," said Chief Abrams rather loudly into his phone. "Give the security guards the go-ahead to help. We don't have a choice, with all the area we have to cover." He hung up and looked at his wife. "I'd better get out to the search area. With all the different departments on this case, I want to be on the ground coordinating everything."

Mrs. Abrams pointed to her cheek. The chief rolled his eyes, then planted an awkward kiss on the spot. His own face turned instantly red, and he marched away.

"Do you think you'll find them?" Felix asked.

Abrams stopped and turned his lumbering frame around. "I just got off the phone with the State Patrol. They've got every resource they have focused on the problem. And we've sent all of ours out, too. Every highway and side road have been checked within the perimeter we've set up, and law enforcement is moving out methodically through the Catskill Mountains trying to find those darned toys. What more do you want from me?" He let out a grunt, like a hoofed animal might, then turned and marched down the hall.

Mrs. Abrams turned back to the kids. "You may not know it, but my husband was thankful for your help."

"He actually told you that?" Gertie asked.

"Not in so many words. But I know. A wife always knows. I will work on him and see if he can be a little more understanding toward you kids in the future. But I am sure you came to see Timmy, right? You go on in." Mrs. Abrams looked at her watch. "I have some last-minute Christmas details to attend to anyway." She wished them a Merry Christmas and headed for the stairs at the other end of the hall.

"I like her," said Gertie.

"Yeah," said Charlotte. "I do too."

"So how can she be married to that blustering fool of a chief?" Gertie asked.

"Don't you think that's a little harsh?" Stanley said.

"Okay, he's not *always* blustering," Gertie said with a sassy smile.

Stanley opened the door to the hospital room. Inside, Officer Evans, a woman, and a little girl were sitting around the bed of a little boy.

Evans smiled when the kids entered. "You kids didn't have to... Look, son, you have visitors."

The little boy looked their way, but he didn't smile. Stanley didn't know what to do.

But Felix spotted the food tray. "Hey, Timmy," he said, "I bet you never saw someone eat Jell-O through their nose before."

The little boy's eyes brightened a little.

Felix walked over to the food tray, sat on the side of the bed, and performed his trick. Before long, Timmy was giggling. He leaned over to his dad and whispered something.

Felix leaned back and cracked his knuckles. "He loved it and he wants me to do it again, am I right?"

"Actually," said Evans, "he asked me why you smell like dirty shoes."

Gertie exploded in laughter, and when she did, little Timmy did as well. Before long, the whole room was laughing. Everybody, that is, except for Felix.

"Thanks for coming, guys," Evans finally said. "We haven't laughed like that in a long time."

"Yeah," said Stanley, "well, Felix usually has that effect on people."

Felix scratched his chin. "I'm supposed to be offended by all of this, right?"

Laughter erupted once again.

Stanley was about to say his goodbyes when Charlotte stepped in front of him, walked over to Timmy's bed, and sat down. "I'll tell you what *really* stinks. You having to be here during Christmas."

Timmy looked down. "Yeah, it does."

"I know how it feels."

"To be in the hospital?"

She shook her head. "No... but Christmas is kinda

hard for me, too." She looked away, and Stanley could see the pain in her eyes.

Mrs. Evans exchanged a look with her husband.

Charlotte's voice was quiet. "It makes me think about my mom. I wonder if she's okay. I wonder if she can see me. If she knows how I'm doing."

Timmy locked eyes with Charlotte. "Your mom, she's—"

"She's gone," Charlotte said quietly. "She died just after Christmas when I was little. And you know what? I'd give all the presents I've ever had in my life just to have one more day with her. Just her and my dad and me. Together again."

Mrs. Evans dabbed at her eyes.

"So Timmy, I know what you're going through is rough, and I know you're sick, and I know this Christmas isn't what you were hoping for. But believe me, your mom and dad and sister love you so much. And in the end, that's what matters most."

Mrs. Evans put her arms around Charlotte, andto Stanley's surprise, Charlotte didn't pull away.

Then Stanley heard something he didn't think he'd ever heard in his life.

Charlotte was crying.

Stanley looked at the others and motioned to the door with his head. He, Gertie, Felix, and Herman walked out into the hall and left Charlotte alone.

"So," said Stanley, "I'll wait for Charlotte. You guys go on home."

"And if you hear something...?" Gertie said.

"I'll send everyone a text. Promise."

The others took off. A few minutes later the door opened and Charlotte stepped into the hall. They walked home from the hospital without saying a word.

When they got to Stanley's house, he hesitated.

"So... are you okay?" he said.

She nodded.

"You know, you could always—"

"I'm fine, Stanley, really. You'll call me as soon as you hear?"

"Promise."

But Stanley had a sinking feeling that he wouldn't be hearing anything for the rest of the night. At least, not anything good.

CHAPTER ELEVEN

CHARCOAL FOR CHRISTMAS

Stanley stomped his boots on the welcome mat and unzipped his coat.

"Stanley, is that you?"

"Yeah, Mom." He walked into the kitchen, where his mom was chopping vegetables. "Did you hear about what happened at Mr. Douglas's Toy Store today?"

She nodded. "I called your father and let him know. Everyone's just sick about it. I suppose that's what you've been up to all day?"

"Yeah."

Stanley's mom bent down and gave him a hug. "I probably don't tell you this enough, but I'm proud of you. Sometimes I worry about that big brain of yours. Then I remember that you have the heart to match it."

Stanley smiled.

His mom stepped back and put her hands on her hips. "But don't think that's getting you out of helping me get this house ready. Now go upstairs and clean up. Then I need your help wiping down the good silverware before your grandmother chastises me for not taking care of her good silver."

Stanley's little sister, Rachel, skipped into the kitchen. "Then you can help me set the table. Mom's getting the Christmas dishes out of the hutch. And I get to fold the napkins this year."

"Okay," Stanley said with a laugh. "I'll be quick."

He went upstairs to his room, hung his coat on a bedpost, and looked at the wrapped presents for his family piled on the dresser. He'd take them down and put them under the tree before tackling the silverware.

As he pulled his wallet from his pocket to set it on his desk, two other objects fell to the floor. One was the Grinch's "You Stink" note that had led them down the sewers. The other object was long and wrapped in a paper menu. Where did that come from?

He unwrapped the menu. Inside was Herman's pencil, the one he'd used to make the map. And there was a note scribbled on the menu. It read:

Stanley,

> *Thanks for letting me hang out with you guys.*
> *Merry Christmas,*
> *Herman*
> *P.S. Charcoal pencils make everyone a better artist!*

Stanley smiled.

He bent over and picked up the note from the Grinch. The smile left his face as he examined it. He had hoped this note would lead them to the stolen toys, but instead all it had done was lead them on a wild goose chase. A dead end.

The frustrations of the day all rushed together at that moment. Stanley tossed the note angrily at the trashcan. It hit the rim and fell to the floor. Stanley slumped into his desk chair and buried his face in his hands. Another failure.

Just then the doorbell rang.

I'd better get a move on, he thought. *Grandparents are here, and the silverware needs de-smudging.*

As he rose wearily from his chair, a knock sounded at his bedroom door.

"I'm coming, Mom."

"It's not your mom, Stanley," said a familiar voice.

Stanley flew across the room and opened the door. "Charlotte? Is everything okay?"

"No, it's not. Nothing about this case is okay. And I'm not going home till we—there's *got* to be something we've missed, Stanley. And *you're* going to figure out what it is."

Stanley shook his head. "No. I'm not. Evans was right. We've done everything we can, and now the police are searching the Catskills for those toys. They might find them, they might not. But all we can do—all *I* can do—is wait."

Charlotte folded her arms and growled through her teeth. "I'm not waiting. Now run it through, Stanley."

"Charlotte, it's no use. We did the math, and it led

us to the boat and the train, both of which ended up being the wrong path!"

"And you don't find that strange?" Charlotte asked.

"I find it incredibly frustrating," said Stanley. "And the only evidence we have has been just as frustrating."

He bent over and grabbed the Grinch's note off the floor. "None of the math or any of the Grinch's clues have helped us get any closer to those toys."

Stanley's phone rang. It was Evans. Stanley hit the speaker button. "Any news?"

"Well, it's not good news, but it *is* news."

"What is it?"

"We must be on the right track, because one of the officers found a note attached to a tree. The note said:

Then the Whos down in Whoville
will all cry BOO-HOO!

Stanley sighed. "It's from *How the Grinch Stole Christmas*! It's when the Grinch describes how his victims will feel Christmas morning when they don't have presents. This guy is something else. And I forgot to tell you, but we found a similar piece of paper at Douglas's and forgot to give it to you. Think it'll turn up any clues?"

"Probably not. These guys are good. They would have wiped it clean. Besides, everybody at the station is out on patrol. They're closed down like every other place in town. I just tried to get another present for Timmy, but this whole place is a ghost town. I'm headed back to the hospital now."

"Well, for what it's worth," said Stanley, "I wish you and your family a Merry Christmas."

"Thanks, Stanley."

Stanley flipped his phone shut. "You're welcome to stay for dinner, Charlotte—"

She held up a finger. She was holding the Grinch's note under Stanley's lamp and looking intently at it.

"Do you see this?" she said without taking her eyes off the paper.

"What?" Stanley asked.

"I swear I felt something at the bottom of the page. Under the lamp, it looks like—wait. Here, sit down and see if you can make anything out."

Stanley sat down and moved his eyes slowly over the bottom couple of inches of the back of the paper. Then he felt it with his fingertips.

"I don't know," he said. "Maybe. There aren't any marks, but there might be..."

"Impressions," said Charlotte. "Very faint impressions." Her eyes widened. "As if someone had written something on *another* piece of paper over this one, and this one picked up the imprint. But of what?"

"Let's see, shall we?"

Stanley had seen this trick once on a TV show. He took Herman's charcoal pencil, held it sideways, and lightly brushed it across the paper. And slowly, something started to appear. Stanley grabbed a pen and went over the faint lines.

They weren't just lines.

They were numbers.

Lots of numbers.

He and Charlotte tried to make sense of what they saw. Numbers were Stanley's life. But were these numbers random, or did they mean something?

"41.77974 – 74.16415," Charlotte said. "A subtraction problem? What does it mean?"

"I have no idea. But let's do the problem." Stanley closed his eyes for a long moment, then opened them. "The answer is negative 32.3844." He frowned at Charlotte. "What the heck is 'negative 32.3844' supposed to mean?"

Charlotte chewed on her lip as she studied the note. Then suddenly she smiled. "It doesn't mean anything, Stanley. This isn't a subtraction problem at all. We missed something. Look, you can barely see it, but right here between the numbers... *this* is a comma."

Stanley leaned in and looked just to the left of the minus sign. "I'm not so sure."

"I am," said Charlotte. "And I think I know what these numbers might be, I just can't figure out how they fit the crime. Stanley, run it through again."

"No, Charlotte, I told you. I'm not going over the math again. It's all been right and you know it. And it's gotten us nowhere. The Grinch has been flaunting our math in our faces all day, and I'm not playing his little game anymore. He's a world-class jerk. I mean, who does this kind of thing on Christmas Eve? People were counting on giving those toys to their kids as Christmas gifts, and now there isn't even time for them to buy their kids anything else! Just like Mabel said, everything's closed. The diner, the general store, the bank, all of Main Street closed at three o'clock. Ravensburg is a ghost town. You saw what this has done to—"

Charlotte grabbed him by the arm. "Wait a second! Stanley, that's it!"

"What?"

"What have we been doing all day long?"

"How many more times do I need to say it? We've been on a wild goose chase. The math has been right and the answers have led us all wrong. Someone's been messing with us all day, Charlotte."

"Exactly," said Charlotte. "And I just figured out

why. And I absolutely *know* what these numbers are!"

She took out her cell phone and punched the digits into the keypad. "This little mark is definitely a comma, which means this isn't a subtraction problem. It's a set of numbers." She looked at the screen, smiled broadly, then turned the phone toward Stanley.

On the screen was a map of Ravensburg with a red flag hovering over Douglas's Toy Store. Stanley studied it in silence for a full minute before he understood. "The numbers are GPS coordinates?"

"Yes," said Charlotte. "We need to call Evans. Now."

"Why?" Stanley said. "How does this help us? These numbers must have been written by the thieves for their hit on the toy store this morning."

"Maybe," said Charlotte. "But Stanley, listen to me. Do you remember when we were geocaching that one day out near Farmer Dahlgren's place? Don't you remember the difference between using GPS coordinates to five decimal places as opposed to only four decimal places?"

"Yeah," said Stanley. "Your phone only calculates GPS to the fourth decimal place. We had trouble finding that geocache until we used Felix's GPS monitor."

Charlotte's smile grew wider. "And how many decimal places do *these* GPS coordinates have?"

Stanley looked at the note. "Five," he said.

"Which means...?"

Stanley pushed his glasses up the bridge of his nose. He thought about what had been bothering him all day—why were these toys so valuable? And then all at once, it hit him.

"This was never about the toys," he said.

Charlotte smiled her biggest smile yet. "Call Evans. Now."

CHAPTER TWELVE

BOOM!

Eleven minutes later, at 4:30 p.m., Stanley, Charlotte, Gertie, Felix, Herman, and Officer Bobby Evans stood in the middle of an empty Douglas's Toy Store. All of Main Street was dead quiet.

"This had better be important," said Gertie. "I had what I'm pretty sure was the beginnings of a royal flush against Granny."

"You were playing poker with your grandma?" Herman asked.

"And the pot's over twenty bucks!" Gertie said. "I can buy a complete zombie makeup kit with twenty bucks. So, Stanley, what is it?"

Stanley held up a piece of paper. "It's this. Charlotte discovered something at the bottom of the Grinch's note. An impression on the paper. So I penciled over it with a charcoal pencil." He smiled at Herman. "That revealed these numbers. They're GPS coordinates that *seemed* to be for this toy store."

"That doesn't help much, Stanley," said Evans, taking the paper. "Seeing as how they *already* robbed this store."

Gertie took the paper from Evans. "But wait— why use GPS? Douglas's has an address."

Herman took the paper from Gertie. "They probably used GPS because they were traveling underground in the sewers. GPS was the surest way of getting to the right spot."

"Exactly," said Stanley.

Felix took the paper from Herman. "But still, we already know they robbed the store, so why does this even matter?"

"Because of the burning question that won't go away," said Stanley. "Why go to all this trouble to steal Douglas's toys?"

"Because they're great toys," Felix and Gertie said together.

"Right, but are they really *that* valuable? What if,

just for a moment, we consider that maybe none of this was really about the toys?"

Felix, Gertie, and Herman all exchanged a confused look.

"Officer Evans," said Charlotte, "where are the Ravensburg police right now?"

"As I've told you, every police resource we have, and I mean *every* off-duty officer, highway patrolman, and security guard, is tracking these guys in the Catskills. In fact, I might be the only one within forty miles of Ravensburg right now—" Evans looked at Stanley and Charlotte with sudden understanding.

Charlotte nodded. "It wasn't the toys that were valuable. It was getting everyone *looking* for the toys that was valuable."

"Your math may have been right today," said Evans, "but our guesses have been wrong. How do you know your guess is right this time?"

"Because of extra credit." Stanley smiled. "It's like those math word problems where they give you a whole bunch of information, and you need to figure out what's important and what's superfluous.

Once we cleared away the superfluous information, it was really quite simple."

"Superfluous?" Herman said.

"You know, extra information that's not important. The Grinch gave us a problem with a bunch of extra information that wasn't important so we wouldn't focus in on his real goal. He knew that taking the toys was the best way of guaranteeing the cops would focus all their efforts on an elaborate chase through the region—tying up as much of the police force as possible."

"So, Three-Card Monte again?" Herman said.

Stanley nodded.

"You're saying they were after another target the whole time?" Gertie asked. "What were they really after?"

"To answer that," said Stanley, "we need to have some clarity on what the GPS coordinates are really pointing to. I asked Felix to bring his GPS monitor along for a more accurate reading. Felix?"

Felix held the monitor with one hand and entered the numbers with his thumb. "Just about... There. Okay."

"Does it point here just like we thought?" Gertie asked.

Felix looked up from his GPS monitor. "Well, um... not exactly."

Gertie looked over his shoulder. "What do you mean, not exactly?"

"By the looks of it, I'd say these GPS coordinates point to a spot about thirty feet that way." Felix pointed to a wall about fifteen feet away.

"Well then you're wrong, because you just pointed to a wall," said Gertie.

"What lies on the other side of that wall?" Stanley asked.

Evans's eyes widened. "It's the bank!"

"Bingo," said Stanley. "When Charlotte and I first discovered these numbers and she punched them into her phone, we figured they just pointed to the toy store. You remember how we were geocaching ? We figured something out that day. As long as we used Charlotte's phone and followed the GPS coordinates to the fourth decimal, we could only find the *approximate* area for the geocache. It wasn't until we used Felix's GPS monitor and followed the coordinates to the fifth decimal that we were able to narrow in on the exact tree."

"Wait a second," said Gertie. "The GPS coordinates were pointing to the bank the whole time?"

"I get it!" said Herman. "The thieves are traveling through the sewers. They'll rob the bank and get away the same way before the police even know what happened."

Evans put a hand to his head. "Every law enforcement officer is out in the Catskill Mountains while the guys we *should* be looking for will be in the sewers under Ravensburg. These guys cleared us out of the way so that no one can stop them."

Stanley nodded. "It's a brilliant plan, really. There's nobody at all around for miles. Everything in town closed at three today. And when the bank alarms go off, every cop will be forty miles away."

"Not every cop," said Evans, taking his gun from its holster. "You kids stay here. I'm—"

BOOOOOM!

The floor and walls of the building shook, knocking them all off their feet. Alarm bells sounded.

"What in the heck was that?" Gertie squealed.

Herman was already moving. "Explosives! I bet somebody just blew a hole in the underside of the bank."

The kids and Officer Evans ran downstairs, found the manhole cover, and opened it. Evans put his finger to his lips, signaled for absolute quiet, and motioned for them to stay put. Then he climbed down into the sewer and ran toward the explosion.

After a minute, Stanley heard the faint sound of voices. Then a lot of yelling. And over it all, he heard a single, clear voice.

"Police! Put your hands up where I can see them!"

More screaming. More noise.

And all at once, Stanley and the others couldn't stay put any longer. They climbed down into the sewer and ran toward the commotion, with Charlotte leading the way.

But by the time they turned the corner in the sewer tunnel, it was all over. Officer Evans was waving his gun at seven rough-looking men, who stepped slowly out from behind several wooden wagons—much sturdier wagons than the ones the kids had found that afternoon. In the back of each wagon was a large black metal safe. And above their heads was an enormous hole in the bottom of the bank building. Bits of concrete and dust lay everywhere.

Officer Evans handcuffed one of the men, then tied the other men's hands with their own belts—and tied their shoelaces together for good measure.

The caper was foiled. But there was still one problem. They'd stopped the thieves... but they still hadn't recovered the missing toys.

Evans implored and even threatened the men to reveal where the presents were hidden, but all seven of the thieves decided to respect their right to remain silent and wait for their lawyer. Evans finally gave up, called for backup, walked the thieves out of the sewer through Douglas's Toy Store, and sat them outside to wait.

Half an hour later, Chief Abrams and four police cruisers came streaking through town with their lights and sirens blaring. They hauled the thieves to jail, and both Ravensburg Bank President Bob Hazelnutt and Mr. Douglas were called to the scene.

Mr. Hazelnutt stared at the hole in complete disbelief.

"How much was in the safe tonight?" Evans asked.

"Five and a half million dollars." Hazelnutt could barely get the words out.

Evans turned to Stanley. "Now we know why the thieves went to so much trouble. That's a lot of money." He shook his head. "You kids did amazing work today. I thank you. I just... I just wish we had recovered the toys. If only we knew where the thieves hid them."

Stanley smiled. "Actually, Officer Evans, I think I know *exactly* where they hid those toys."

Evans's eyes widened. "What? You do?"

"I do. I bet the thieves just wanted us to *think* they had the toys this whole time. They made those heavy drag marks, footprints, and tire treads just to make us believe they had the toys—so we'd go chasing them all over."

"Then where *are* the toys?" Evans asked.

Stanley's smile grew bigger. "You're not big on waiting either, are you?"

The door of the bank flew open, and Herman entered, carrying a large black sack. Felix and the girls followed, each dragging a huge sack as well.

"We found the toys!" cried Charlotte. "There's another twelve of these back in the sewers. The thieves threw them way down a side tunnel. We didn't think to search there this morning because there were no footprints."

Felix pumped his fist in the air. "We saved Christmas. We actually *saved Christmas*! Think they'll make a movie about us someday? Once Brad Pitt's schedule opens up to play yours truly, I mean?"

The kids laid the sacks at Mr. Douglas's feet. The toymaker looked at them through misty eyes. "How can I ever begin to thank you?"

Felix reached into his back pocket. "Funny you should ask." He handed Mr. Douglas a piece of paper. "It's called a Kid-A-Pult, and those are detailed blueprints."

Mr. Douglas took out his reading glasses and looked over the crayon drawing on the back of the paper menu. He peeked over his glasses and smiled. "Not a chance, Felix. But you might all wake up tomorrow to find a little something under your trees that isn't from Santa."

Mr. Douglas turned to Officer Evans. "Bobby, I know your boy's in the hospital this Christmas. Would you mind helping me take the toys up there?"

"Be my pleasure, Mr. Douglas." Evans grabbed a sack and started toward the door. Then he stopped and turned back. "Charlotte?" he said. "We're going to need some help handing out these toys. Do you think maybe...?"

"I'd love to," said Charlotte, grinning.

"I think we all would," Stanley added.

The next hour was a flurry of activity, excitement, hugs, and even a few tears. The Math Inspectors and their families, along with Herman and Officer Evans, helped Mr. Douglas deliver the greatest toys in the world to the boys and girls in Ravensburg Hospital.

And they served a very special present last, to the very special boy at the end of floor two.

It was Charlotte and her dad who handed Timmy his beautifully wrapped present.

"Well, don't you want to open it?" Charlotte asked.

Timmy looked around his room at all the smiling faces. "Mr. Douglas, if it's all right, I kind of want to wait till tomorrow. It'll make waking up Christmas morning fun, even in the hospital."

Mr. Douglas looked at all the families around him. "That's a great idea. Christmas morning should be just as wonderful as this Christmas Eve has ended up being."

When the visitors made it out of the hospital, the parents started for home and left the kids to say their goodbyes.

An expensive-looking red car honked, and Herman waved at it. "That's my ride, guys. I'd better get going. But first..." He patted his pockets and fished out an envelope. He handed it to Felix.

"Is this a card?" Felix asked. "For me?"

"Listen, Felix, the way you were teasing me today... it made me feel like I was really one of the gang. And I just wanted to let you know how much I appreciate it."

Felix looked genuinely touched. He ripped open the envelope and took out a red and green greeting card. He cleared his throat. "The Merriest Of Christmases, from Your Friend, *Mr....*"

Felix opened up the card, and a small brown figure popped out at him just as he said the word "*Squirrel.*" He screamed, threw the card into the street, and fell into a heap on the sidewalk.

"Why you dirty, low-down... I oughta..."

Herman held out his hand. "No hard feelings, eh, Felix?"

Felix took Herman's hand and stumbled back to his feet. "I guess not."

"Oh, that reminds me," Herman said.

He waved again at the driver of the vehicle, who opened the door and jogged across the street. It was a man in his mid-thirties with nice clothes and an elegant look about him.

The man walked up to them and stuck out his hand. "I'm Farley Dale," he said. "Nice to meet you."

Felix's eyes about popped out of his head. "You mean the show-chicken-raising, animal-trapping Uncle Farley?"

The man gave Felix a most peculiar look.

Herman put an arm around Felix's shoulders. "Whatever are you talking about, Felix? Uncle Farley is a distinguished professor of Art History at the local college. After school he tutors at-risk kids, and he sings in his local church. Oh, and he and his wife are expecting their second baby in the spring."

"But you said he... argghhh. So you don't go boating on the Hudson?"

"All the time," said Uncle Farley. "I'm a bird watcher. I take photos for the National Audubon Society."

Felix's face twisted in confusion. Then, finally, his eyes opened wide and he pointed at Herman. "You! You... were messing with me?"

Herman winked, and a big smile spread across his face. "It would appear I was. Merry Christmas, Felix."

Herman and Uncle Farley took off, and Felix was left stammering and spluttering in the middle of the sidewalk.

"You know what?" Gertie said. "I think I'm going to like having Herman around." She punched Felix in the shoulder. "Come on, you big lug. Time to walk me home."

As Felix and Gertie headed off in one direction, Charlotte and Stanley set off in another. And they did so in silence. Not a glum silence, but a contented silence. The kind that two friends can share. They listened to the crunch of the snow under their feet, the sound of Christmas music coming from people's houses, the sounds of guests arriving for Christmas Eve parties.

Finally they stopped outside Stanley's house.

"You did really good today, Charlotte," said Stanley.

"*We* did good today, Stanley. It was a team effort."

"Those kids sure looked happy."

"Yeah, they did. And that felt good."

"So, you and your dad?"

"We'll be all right. You gotta stop worrying about me."

"You know you're more than welcome to spend Christmas Eve with—"

"Thanks, Stanley. I know. But you know my dad, and that would never happen."

"Actually... you're wrong," Stanley said, a grin spreading across his face. "He already did."

"What?"

"My folks talked to your dad at the hospital. Your dad already said yes. My mom told me to tell you that you're expected to show up at our house in exactly one hour, wearing your very best Christmas dress. And if you're back before that, I might even let you help me polish the silverware."

Charlotte grew quiet, and Stanley could swear he saw her eyes get wet again. Then she nodded and said, "Thank you. For everything."

She wheeled around and started to jog home.

Stanley walked up the sidewalk to his house. Just

as he reached his porch, he heard his name.

"Stanley!"

He turned around. Charlotte was wearing the largest, prettiest smile he'd ever seen in his life.

"Yes?"

"Merry Christmas, Stanley Robinson Carusoe! Merry Christmas!"

CHAPTER THIRTEEN

EPILOGUE

The text arrived at 7:15 a.m. the day after Christmas. A group text, sent by Felix.

"EMERGENCY MEETING!
TREEHOUSE! ASAP!!!!!"

Charlotte and Stanley reached Felix's house just as Herman and Gertie arrived from the other direction. Felix was pacing in front of the treehouse ladder.

"Felix, what's wrong?" Gertie asked.

"Wrong?" he said. "I ask you a question. Did any of you receive your promised present from Mr. Douglas yesterday morning?"

One by one they each answered no.

"Felix," said Gertie, "who really cares? Don't you think poor Mr. Douglas had more important things to do?"

Felix stopped. "No, as a matter of fact, I do not." Then a grin spread across his face. "And apparently, neither did he."

Stanley and Charlotte shared a confused look. It was at that moment that Felix stepped aside and pointed to something on the ground on the other side of the treehouse.

There, in the middle of Felix's back yard, sat the largest cardboard box any of them had ever seen, topped with an enormous red bow.

"I saw it out my window this morning. The note on it says, 'To: The Math Inspectors.'"

The kids ran around the treehouse and reached the present together.

Felix took control. "Grab hold. Okay, on my count."

"Herman," Gertie said. "Get over here."

Herman put his hands in his pockets. "But it says it's for the Math Inspectors."

"Exactly," said Stanley. "So get over here."

Herman smiled and took his place with the others.

"Okay guys," screamed Felix. "On one, two, three!"

They all moved in different directions, and as the cardboard fell to the ground, Mr. Douglas's present emerged.

Felix screamed and fell to his knees.

"OH MY KID-A-PULT!"

Oh my Kid-A-Pult was right. Mr. Douglas had apparently had himself a very busy Christmas Day. Stanley had never seen anything like it. And as the kids touched every nook and cranny of the complicated contraption, Felix declared that from now on, the day the Kid-A-Pult was built would be considered a national holiday.

When Gertie informed him that it already was— and it was called "Christmas"—Felix nodded and said with a satisfied grin, "Even better."

The first testing of the Kid-A-Pult happened at exactly 7:47. By Stanley's estimate, Felix was thrown seventy-five feet. He landed in a deep snowdrift in the middle of Howie Lattner's back yard.

Felix declared it the finest moment of his life.

And that's when Charlotte had a brilliant idea. "You know what, guys? If the song is right, there are twelve days of Christmas. But it really sounded to me like Polly's idea of a Christmas season truce was a one-day sort of thing."

"That is what she said," said Stanley.

Gertie clapped her hands. "*And* she was silly enough to announce to the world *exactly* where she'd be today at 'noontide.'"

Charlotte nodded. "You know... I bet the Kid-A-Pult could chuck snowballs a really, *really* long way."

Herman knocked on the giant wheels at the base of the contraption. "It does seem to be mobile."

"I think dodging snowballs might spice up Polly's performance," said Gertie. "Stanley, what do you think?"

"I'm in. But I think we're going to have to ask Felix. I mean, Polly *is* his future girlfriend after all, and the Kid-A-Pult *was* delivered to his yard, so..."

"Use my Kid-A-Pult in an act of war against the forces of English?" said Felix. "Who am I to get in the way of progress?"

"Really?" Gertie asked.

Felix went to the front of the Kid-A-Pult, grabbed the rope attached to it, and put it over his shoulder. "And for the record, if Polly asks whether it was me throwing snowballs at her during her performance..."

"You'll own up to it?"

"Not a chance. I'm blaming it all on Uncle Farley. Come on, Math Inspectors, we've got a job to do."

CHAPTER FOURTEEN

MEANWHILE

"I can help the next person," said the librarian. She pulled a single book across the scanner and looked closely at the front cover. "Last year's Ravensburg Elementary School yearbook, huh? Do you know somebody who went there?"

The library patron smiled. "Several students, actually, though not as well as I would like. I am starting a sort of life lessons internship, and I am researching a few promising candidates."

"What a wonderful idea," said the librarian. "I wish more people would give back to the community like that. Well, this book should help you get started. It's due back in thirty days."

The patron placed the book in a leather case, walked to the coffee shop next door, and sat down at a secluded table near the fireplace.

"Coffee?" asked a waiter.

"Yes. But you better bring a thermos of it; I am going to be here a while."

The waiter nodded. "You're the boss."

The patron smiled as if something was funny, then opened the yearbook to the index, ran a finger down the page, and stopped at: Carusoe, Stanley. "Well, Math Inspectors, you have just become worthy of my notice. The game is afoot."

END OF BOOK THREE

BONUS MATH PROBLEMS...

Do You Have What It Takes
To Be A Math Inspector?

Hi, fellow Math Inspectors, it's Gertie here!

Well, for the third time in a row now, Felix and I have gotten stuck putting together some word problems to help sharpen your skills. Not that I mind it, of course. My only question is when do we stop calling these things "Math Inspectors Word Problems" and start calling them "Gertie and Felix Are Awesome Problems Because They Do All The Work"?

Okay, maybe that would be a little long. But I'll be thinking it from now on.

So, I asked Felix how he wanted to handle things this time, and he told me to go fishing. At first I took it as an insult. Then I realized he *actually* wanted me to go fishing with him. And seeing as how it's the middle of winter, the only fishing people do around here is ice fishing.

Now, this may come as a surprise to you all since I'm such a sportswoman, but I detest fishing. And since Felix has been trying to get me to go fishing with him for years, I'm pretty sure this is just a ploy to get me out on Lake Ravensburg in late December. And since I'm right outside his freezing, stinking ice fish hut now, a math problem occurs to me.

Word Problem #1 — You know how boring fishing is? I'll rate it a 98 out of 100 on the boring scale. In fact, the only thing more boring than fishing is watching Polly and the English Club perform a play. If Felix gets pulled into the water by an enormous fish for just long enough to make his teeth chatter all the way back home to his hot chocolate, it will make fishing today only half as boring as usual. So here's the question: if Felix takes a short ice bath, how boring will fishing be today on the old boring scale?

Howdy, fellow fishermen, it's Felix. So listen to this: I've been trying to get Gertie to come ice fishing with me since we were like two years old. And I finally did it! Of course, to do so, I had to tell her we could work on the math problems out here. It's worth it though. Seeing her in an ice hut is priceless.

Get this. I hooked one right before she got here, and as soon as she came in I handed her the pole and said I had to go do something outside. Which I do. I have to give you all the next word problem, because I wasn't lying about the math you can find in fishing. It's everywhere.

Word Problem #2 — I would rate fishing a 98 out of 100 on the excitement scale. In fact, only watching Polly perform a play is more— What did you say, Gertie? You've already done a problem like this? Oh. Well, no problem, folks. As I said, math is everywhere in fishing. I've got plenty more where that came from.

Okay, let's see. So a fishing license around here costs $10 for a kid. If you get caught fishing without a license, the park ranger makes you pay the full price of the license, plus an additional penalty of 130% of the original price of a license. What is the total amount of money Gertie will have to pay when I call my dad's buddy, the park ranger, and tell him Gertie is fishing without a license today?

It's Gertie again! Turns out fishing is the greatest thing in the world, and I'm a natural at it! Not only did I land the fish that Felix was having so much trouble with, but I have since pulled four more whoppers out of this tiny hole in the ice. I have to admit, it's a little freaky being separated from freezing cold water by only a few inches of frozen water, but as long as Felix baits the hooks and takes the fish off when they come in, I could get used to this. Probably because I'm so good at it. And I've got statistical proof I'm good, because I asked Felix how many fish he got last week, and... actually, let's compare our natural abilities in a word problem, shall we?

Word Problem #3 —Last week Felix came out to Lake Ravensburg for a whole day of fishing with his dad. Felix only caught two fish that whole day. In just the little time I've been here today, I've caught *five* fish and have another on the line now. Youch, this one's a fighter. Counting this one, I've caught six fish and Felix has only caught two.

Now here's your fill-in-the-blank question:

Therefore I, the greatest fisherwoman on earth, have caught _____ % more fish than Felix.

It's me, Felix. We're at Gertie's house now, and she's in the other room thawing out. It was a crazy thing to watch. See, the first five fish Gertie caught were about the size of your little finger. She was really proud, so I didn't want to tell her that all she did was catch fish so small she could have used them as bait to catch real fish. Anyway, that last one she hooked was a different story. Maybe the rumors of a Loch Ravensburg Monster (most of us call her Ravey) are true. Because whatever was on the other end of that line, it was huge.

When I saw that this one was going to be a struggle, I tried to take the fishing pole back. But Gertie didn't let me, and before you know it, she got half pulled into the water and *still* wouldn't let go.

To make matters worse, the park ranger came in at that moment and gave her a ticket for fishing without a license. At least that made her mad enough to let go of the fishing pole.

Anyway, her teeth chattered all the way back home, but now she's warming up over a nice cup of hot chocolate. She *did* manage to give me one more word problem though. I'll skip the chattering sounds she made between every word and just give you the problem.

Word Problem #4 — Fishing is the worst thing in the world, and only doofuses do it. If I charge Felix 25 cents per hour for the honor of shoveling my family's driveway this winter, how many hours will he have to shovel in order to pay off my fishing license and the ticket I got today when the park ranger "mysteriously" appeared out of nowhere to penalize me for doing something I'm never going to do again?

Felix here again, and I detect some hostility from my little friend, so I will make sure the last word problem really cheers her up.

Word Problem #5 — In the spirit of winter, I would like to talk about penguins—specifically the emperor penguin. The average adult emperor penguin is 4 feet and 0 inches tall. Another very interesting fact is that the average twelve-year-old Gertie is only 4 feet and 9 inches tall. Expressed in terms of feet, how many feet taller is the average Gertie than the average emperor penguin? (Hint: the answer should be given as a fraction.)

Felix here one last time with an update on Gertie. That last problem did *not* appear to cheer her up after all, and now she's charging toward me while swinging her arms like a wild animal. Man, I love it when penguins get angry. They're so darn cute. Felix out!

To check your answers or to learn more about The Math Inspectors, go to www.TheMathInspectors.com.

GET TWO DANIEL KENNEY STORIES FOR FREE

BUILDING A RELATIONSHIP WITH MY READERS IS THE VERY BEST THING ABOUT WRITING. I OCCASIONALLY SEND NEWSLETTERS WITH DETAILS ON NEW RELEASES, SPECIAL OFFERS, AND OTHER BITS OF NEWS RELATING TO THE MATH INSPECTORS AND MY OTHER BOOKS FOR KIDS.

AND IF YOU SIGN UP TO THIS MAILING LIST, I WILL SEND YOU THIS FREE CONTENT:

1. A FREE COPY OF MY PICTURE BOOK, *WHEN MR. PUSH CAME TO SHOVE.*
2. A FREE COPY OF MY HILARIOUS ILLUSTRATED BOOK FOR YOUNG PEOPLE, *THE BIG LIFE OF REMI MULDOON.*

YOU CAN GET BOTH BOOKS FOR FREE, BY SIGNING UP AT WWW.DANIELKENNEY.COM.

DID YOU ENJOY THIS BOOK? YOU CAN MAKE A BIG DIFFERENCE!

REVIEWS ARE THE MOST POWERFUL TOOL IN MY ARSENAL WHEN IT COMES TO GETTING ATTENTION FOR MY BOOKS. MUCH AS I'D LIKE TO, I AM NOT A BIG NEW YORK PUBLISHER AND I CAN'T TAKE OUT FULL SIZE ADS IN THE NEW YORK TIMES OR GET MYSELF A SPOT ON NATIONAL TELEVISION SHOWS.

BUT I AM HOPING THAT I CAN EARN SOMETHING MUCH MORE POWERFUL THAN THOSE THINGS. SOMETHING THE BIG PUBLISHERS WOULD LOVE TO HAVE.

A COMMITTED AND LOYAL BUNCH OF READERS. HONEST REVIEWS OF MY BOOKS HELP BRING THEM TO THE ATTENTION OF

OTHER READERS. IF YOU'VE ENJOYED THIS BOOK, I'D BE VERY GRATEFUL IF YOU COULD SPEND JUST FIVE MINUTES LEAVING A REVIEW (IT CAN BE AS SHORT AS YOU LIKE) ON THE BOOK'S AMAZON PAGE.

THANK YOU VERY MUCH!

THE MATH INSPECTORS BOOKS

BOOK ONE: THE CASE OF THE
CLAYMORE DIAMOND

BOOK TWO: THE CASE OF THE
MYSTERIOUS MR. JEKYLL

BOOK THREE: THE CASE OF THE
CHRISTMAS CAPER

BOOK FOUR: THE CASE OF THE
HAMILTON ROLLER COASTER

BOOK FIVE: THE CASE OF THE
FORGOTTEN MINE
COMING SOON!

ALSO BY DANIEL KENNEY

THE SCIENCE INSPECTORS SERIES
COMING SOON!

THE HISTORY MYSTERY KIDS SERIES

THE PROJECT GEMINI SERIES

THE BIG LIFE OF REMI MULDOON

TEENAGE TREASURE HUNTER

KATIE PLUMB & THE PENDLETON GANG

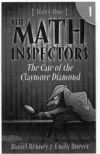

When the Claymore Diamond is stolen from Ravensburg's finest jewelry store, Stanley Carusoe gets the bright idea that he and his friends should start a detective agency.

Armed with curiosity and their love for math, Stanley, Charlotte, Gertie and Felix race around town in an attempt to solve the mystery. Along the way, they butt heads with an ambitious police chief, uncover dark secrets, and drink lots of milkshakes at Mabel's Diner. But when their backs are against the wall, Stanley and his friends rely on the one thing they know best: numbers. Because numbers, they never lie.

Sixth-graders Stanley, Charlotte, Gertie and Felix did more than just start a detective agency. Using their math skills and their gut instincts, they actually solved a crime the police couldn't crack. Now the Math Inspectors are called in to uncover the identity of a serial criminal named Mr. Jekyll, whose bizarre (and hilarious) pranks cross the line into vandalism.

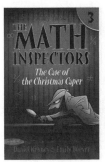

But the deeper the friends delve into the crimes, the more they realize why they were asked to help...and it wasn't because of their detective skills.

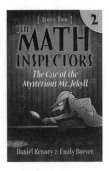

It's Christmas Eve in Ravensburg, and the town is bursting with anticipation for its oldest Christmas tradition. The annual opening of Douglas and Son's Toy Store, home of the greatest toys in the world, is finally here. But this is no ordinary Christmas Eve, and the surprise that awaits them is beyond any of their wildest imaginations: a surprise that threatens to ruin Christmas!

Stanley, Charlotte, Gertie and Felix call in a little backup, but will the team's detective skills and math smarts be enough to unravel the mystery?

Summer vacation has finally arrived, and the Math Inspectors deserve a break. After all, their sixth-grade year was a busy one. On top of all the normal school stuff, Stanley, Charlotte, Gertie, Felix, and Herman made quite a name for themselves as amateur detectives. But when a relaxing day of roller coasters, riddle booths, and waffle eating contests turns into a desperate scramble to save a beloved landmark, the friends quickly discover that this case may be asking more than they are willing to give.

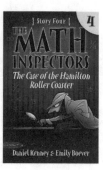

In fact, there may only be one way out—to quit. Will this be the end of the Math Inspectors?

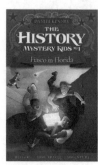

Where did Professor Abner Jefferson go? Before they can find out, April, Henry, and Toad find themselves transported back in time to colonial Florida. Now they have to figure out what's going on, where their father is, and how to get home. Can they find the missing pieces to the puzzle or will they be stuck in history forever?

The History Mystery Kids 1: Fiasco in Florida is the first book in an exciting new time travel series meant for children who have already been reading chapter books and are ready for something more advanced. In each book, this funny, adventuresome series transports children back in time to one of America's 50 states.

The kids at Archie Beller's new school are the weirdest kids in America. Because in Kings Cove, California, kids don't do things like ride bikes, play video games, and read comic books. **Nope, in Kings Cove you're either a Pirate, or you're a Ninja.** And Archie... well, he just wants to be a normal kid from Nebraska. But when these weird kids force Archie to choose a side, **something goes horribly wrong.** Will Archie find his way out of trouble so he can lead the life of a normal kid? Or will he be forced into leading a double life? By day, a normal quiet kid. By night, America's newest crime fighter, a brave superhero known to friend and foe as... PIRATE NINJA!!!

For ten year-old Remi Muldoon, being SMALL is a BIG problem--especially with the kids at school.

And when Remi's attempt to become popular upsets the balance of the universe, things get worse. MUCH worse. Now, Remi must race against the clock to fix history before it's too late and along the way, he might just learn that the smallest of kids can have the biggest of lives.

Brought to life by Author/Illustrator Daniel Kenney, this hilarious first book in the Big Life graphic novel series is perfect for children ages 7-10.

Six months after his mom's death, a still broken-hearted Curial Diggs discovers that she has left him a challenge.

His mom wants him to find The Romanov Dolls, a fantastic treasure stolen from the Manhattan Art Collective when she was only a child. Despite having an overbearing famous father - who has already mapped out his son's future - Curial follows his heart and his mother's clues to Russia where he teams up with the granddaughter of a Russian History Professor to unravel the mystery behind the priceless treasure. Full of history, humor, and danger, Teenage Treasure Hunter is perfect for readers ages 10-14.

ABOUT THE AUTHORS

DANIEL KENNEY

Daniel Kenney is the children's author behind such popular series as *Project Gemini*, *The Big Life of Remi Muldoon*, *The History Mystery Kids*, *The Science Inspectors*, and *The Math Inspectors*. He and his wife live in Omaha, Nebraska, where they enjoy screaming children, little sleep, and dragons. Because who doesn't love dragons? To learn more go to www.DanielKenney.com.

Emily Boever was born with an overactive imagination. She spent much of her childhood convinced she was The Incredible Hulk and adventuring with three imaginary friends. When she grew too old to play with friends no one else could see, she turned her imagination to more mature things like studying, traveling, and teaching. Only after marrying her wonderful husband, Matt, and having kids of her own did Emily discover that she was finally old enough to reunite with her imaginary friends (and even add a few new ones) in the pages of her own books. Emily and Matt live with their kids in Omaha, Nebraska. Find more information at www.EmilyBoever.com.